A Vintage Christmas

A Collection of Classic Stories and Poems

Louisa May Alcott

A Christmas Dream, and how it came

"I'm so tired of Christmas I wish there never would be another one!" exclaimed a discontented-looking little girl, as she sat idly watching her mother arrange a pile of gifts two days before they were to be given.

"Why, Effie, what a dreadful thing to say! You are as bad as old Scrooge; and I 'm afraid something will happen to you, as it did to him, if you don't care for dear Christmas," answered mamma, almost dropping the silver horn she was filling with delicious candies.

"Who was Scrooge? What happened to him?" asked Effie, with a glimmer of interest in her listless face, as she picked out the sourest lemon-drop she could find; for nothing sweet suited her just then.

"He was one of Dickens's best people, and you can read the charming story some day. He hated Christmas until a strange dream showed him how dear and beautiful it was, and made a better man of him."

"I shall read it; for I like dreams, and have a great many curious ones myself. But they don't keep me from being tired of Christmas," said Effie, poking discontentedly among the sweeties for something worth eating.

"Why are you tired of what should be the happiest time of all the year?" asked mamma, anxiously.

"Perhaps I should n't be if I had something new. But it is always the same, and there is n't any more surprise about it. I always find heaps of goodies in my stocking. Don't like some of them, and soon get tired of those I do like. We always have a great dinner, and I eat too much, and feel ill next day. Then

and the other outstretched as if to shower gifts and warmly press all other hands.

Effie forgot to speak as this bright vision came nearer, leaving no trace of footsteps in the snow, only lighting the way with its little candle, and filling the air with the music of its song.

"Dear child, you are lost, and I have come to find you," said the stranger, taking Effie's cold hands in his, with a smile like sunshine, while every holly berry glowed like a little fire.

"Do you know me?" asked Effie, feeling no fear, but a great gladness, at his coming.

"I know all children, and go to find them; for this is my holiday, and I gather them from all parts of the world to be merry with me once a year."

"Are you an angel?" asked Effie, looking for the wings.

"No; I am a Christmas spirit, and live with my mates in a pleasant place, getting ready for our holiday, when we are let out to roam about the world, helping make this a happy time for all who will let us in. Will you come and see how we work?"

"I will go anywhere with you. Don't leave me again," cried Effie, gladly.

"First I will make you comfortable. That is what we love to do. You are cold, and you shall be warm; hungry, and I will feed you; sorrowful, and I will make you gay."

With a wave of his candle all three miracles were wrought,--for the snow-flakes turned to a white fur cloak and hood on Effie's head and shoulders; a bowl of hot soup came sailing to her lips, and vanished when she had eagerly drunk the last drop; and suddenly the dismal field changed to a new world so full of wonders that all her troubles were forgotten in a minute.

Bells were ringing so merrily that it was hard to keep from dancing. Green garlands hung on the walls, and every tree was a Christmas tree full of toys, and blazing with candles that never went out.

In one place many little spirits sewed like mad on warm clothes, turning off work faster than any sewing-machine ever invented, and great piles were made ready to be sent to poor people. Other busy creatures packed money into purses, and wrote checks which they sent flying away on the wind,--a lovely kind of snow-storm to fall into a world below full of poverty.

Older and graver spirits were looking over piles of little books, in which the records of the past year were kept, telling how different people had spent it, and what sort of gifts they deserved. Some got peace, some disappointment, some remorse and sorrow, some great joy and hope. The rich had generous thoughts sent them; the poor, gratitude and contentment. Children had more love and duty to parents; and parents renewed patience, wisdom, and satisfaction for and in their children. No one was forgotten.

"Please tell me what splendid place this is?" asked Effie, as soon as she could collect her wits after the first look at all these astonishing things.

"This is the Christmas world; and here we work all the year round, never tired of getting ready for the happy day. See, these are the saints just setting off; for some have far to go, and the children must not be disappointed."

As he spoke the spirit pointed to four gates, out of which four great sleighs were just driving, laden with toys, while a jolly old Santa Claus sat in the middle of each, drawing on his mittens and tucking up his wraps for a long cold drive.

"Why, I thought there was only one Santa Claus, and even he was a humbug," cried Effie, astonished at the sight.

"Never give up your faith in the sweet old stories, even after you come to see that they are only the pleasant shadow of a lovely truth."

Just then the sleighs went off with a great jingling of bells and pattering of reindeer hoofs, while all the spirits gave a cheer that was heard in the lower world, where people said, "Hear the stars sing."

"I never will say there isn't any Santa Claus again. Now, show me more."

"You will like to see this place, I think, and may learn something here perhaps."

The spirit smiled as he led the way to a little door, through which Effie peeped into a world of dolls. Baby-houses were in full blast, with dolls of all sorts going on like live people. Waxen ladies sat in their parlors elegantly dressed; black dolls cooked in the kitchens; nurses walked out with the bits of dollies; and the streets were full of tin soldiers marching, wooden horses prancing, express wagons rumbling, and little men hurrying to and fro. Shops were there, and tiny people buying legs of mutton, pounds of tea, mites of clothes, and everything dolls use or wear or want.

But presently she saw that in some ways the dolls improved upon the manners and customs of human beings, and she watched eagerly to learn why they did these things. A fine Paris doll driving in her carriage took up a black worsted Dinah who was hobbling along with a basket of clean clothes, and carried her to her journey's end, as if it were the proper thing to do. Another interesting china lady took off her comfortable red cloak and put it round a poor wooden creature done up in a paper shift, and so badly painted that its face would have sent some babies into fits.

"Seems to me I once knew a rich girl who didn't give her things to poor girls. I wish I could remember who she was, and tell her to be as kind as that china doll," said Effie, much touched at the sweet way the pretty creature wrapped up the poor fright, and then ran off in her little gray gown to buy a shiny fowl stuck on a wooden platter for her invalid mother's dinner.

"We recall these things to people's minds by dreams. I think the girl you speak of won't forget this one." And the spirit smiled, as if he enjoyed some joke which she did not see.

A little bell rang as she looked, and away scampered the children into the red-and-green school-house with the roof that lifted up, so one could see how nicely they sat at their desks with mites of books, or drew on the inch-square blackboards with crumbs of chalk.

"They know their lessons very well, and are as still as mice. We make a great racket at our school, and get bad marks every day. I shall tell the girls they had better mind what they do, or their dolls will be better scholars than they are," said Effie, much impressed, as she peeped in and saw no rod in the hand of the little mistress, who looked up and shook her head at the intruder, as if begging her to go away before the order of the school was disturbed.

Effie retired at once, but could not resist one look in at the window of a fine mansion, where the family were at dinner, the children behaved so well at table, and never grumbled a bit when their mamma said they could not have any more fruit.

"Now, show me something else," she said, as they came again to the low door that led out of Doll-land.

"You have seen how we prepare for Christmas; let me show you where we love best to send our good and happy gifts," answered the spirit, giving her his hand again.

"I know. I've seen ever so many," began Effie, thinking of her own Christmases.

"So my little girl wanted to be a Christmas spirit too, and make this a happy day for those who had not as many pleasures and comforts as she has. She likes surprises, and we planned this for you all. She shall play the good fairy, and give each of you something from this tree, after which every one will find her own name on a small tree, and can go to enjoy it in her own way. March by, my dears, and let us fill your hands."

Nobody told them to do it, but all the hands were clapped heartily before a single child stirred; then one by one they came to look up wonderingly at the pretty giver of the feast as she leaned down to offer them great yellow oranges, red apples, bunches of grapes, bonbons, and cakes, till all were gone, and a double row of smiling faces turned toward her as the children filed back to their places in the orderly way they had been taught.

Then each was led to her own tree by the good ladies who had helped mamma with all their hearts; and the happy hubbub that arose would have satisfied even Santa Claus himself,--shrieks of joy, dances of delight, laughter and tears (for some tender little things could not bear so much pleasure at once, and sobbed with mouths full of candy and hands full of toys). How they ran to show one another the new treasures! how they peeped and tasted, pulled and pinched, until the air was full of queer noises, the floor covered with papers, and the little trees left bare of all but candles!

"I don't think heaven can be any gooder than this," sighed one small girl, as she looked about her in a blissful maze, holding her full apron with one hand, while she luxuriously carried sugar-plums to her mouth with the other.

"Is that a truly angel up there?" asked another, fascinated by the little white figure with the wreath on its shining hair, who in some mysterious way had been the cause of all this merry-making.

"I wish I dared to go and kiss her for this splendid party," said a lame child, leaning on her crutch, as she stood near the steps, wondering how it seemed to sit in a mother's lap, as Effie was doing, while she watched the happy scene before her.

Effie heard her, and remembering Tiny Tim, ran down and put her arms about the pale child, kissing the wistful face, as she said sweetly, "You may; but mamma deserves the thanks. She did it all; I only dreamed about it."

Lame Katy felt as if "a truly angel" was embracing her, and could only stammer out her thanks, while the other children ran to see the pretty spirit, and touch her soft dress, until she stood in a crowd of blue gowns laughing as they held up their gifts for her to see and admire.

Mamma leaned down and whispered one word to the older girls; and suddenly they all took hands to dance round Effie, singing as they skipped.

It was a pretty sight, and the ladies found it hard to break up the happy revel; but it was late for small people, and too much fun is a mistake. So the girls fell into line, and marched before Effie and mamma again, to say good-night with such grateful little faces that the eyes of those who looked grew dim with tears. Mamma kissed every one; and many a hungry childish heart felt as if the touch of those tender lips was their best gift. Effie shook so many small hands that her own tingled; and when Katy came she pressed a small doll into Effie's hand, whispering, "You did n't have a single present, and we had lots. Do keep that; it's the prettiest thing I got."

"I will," answered Effie, and held it fast until the last smiling face was gone, the surprise all over, and she safe in her own bed, too tired and happy for anything but sleep.

"Mamma, it *was* a beautiful surprise, and I thank you so much! I don't see how you did it; but I like it best of all the Christmases I ever had, and mean to make one every year. I

LITTLE GRETCHEN AND THE WOODEN SHOE

A CHRISTMAS STORY FOR LITTLE CHILDREN

The following story is one of many which has drifted down to us from the story-loving nurseries and hearthstones of Germany. I cannot recall when I first had it told to me as a child, varied of course by different tellers, but always leaving that sweet, tender impression of God's loving care for the least of his children. I have since read different versions of it in at least a half-dozen story books for children.

Once upon a time, a long time ago, far away across the great ocean, in a country called Germany, there could be seen a small log hut on the edge of a great forest, whose fir-trees extended for miles and miles to the north. This little house, made of heavy hewn logs, had but one room in it. A rough pine door gave entrance to this room, and a small square window admitted the light. At the back of the house was built an old-fashioned stone chimney, out of which in winter usually curled a thin blue smoke, showing that there was not very much fire within.

Small as the house was, it was large enough for the two people who lived in it. I want to tell you a story to-day about these two people. One was an old, gray-haired woman, so old that the little children of the village, nearly half a mile away, often wondered whether she had come into the world with the huge mountains and the great fir-trees, which stood like giants back of her small hut. Her face was wrinkled all over with deep lines, which if the children could only have read aright, would have told them of many years of cheerful, happy, self-sacrifice, of loving, anxious watching beside sick-beds, of quiet endurance of pain, of many a day of hunger and cold, and of a thousand deeds of unselfish love for other people; but, of course, they could not read this strange handwriting. They only knew that she was old and wrinkled, and that she stooped as she walked. None of them seemed to fear her, for her smile was always cheerful, and she had a kindly word for each of them if they chanced to meet her on her way to and from the village. With this old, old woman lived a very little girl. So bright and happy was she that the travelers who passed by the lonesome little house on the edge of the forest often thought of a sunbeam as they saw her. These two people were known in the village as Granny Goodyear and Little Gretchen.

The winter had come and the frost had snapped off many of the smaller branches from the pine-trees in the forest. Gretchen and her Granny were up by daybreak each morning. After their simple breakfast of oatmeal, Gretchen would run to the little closet and fetch Granny's old woolen shawl, which seemed almost as old as Granny herself. Gretchen always claimed the right to put the shawl over her Granny's head, even though she had to climb onto the wooden bench to do it. After carefully pinning it under Granny's chin, she gave her a good by kiss, and Granny started out for her morning's work in the forest. This work was nothing more nor less than the gathering up of the twigs and branches which the autumn winds and winter frosts had thrown upon the ground. These were carefully gathered into a large bundle which Granny tied together with a strong linen band. She then managed to lift the bundle to her shoulder and trudged off to the village with it. Here she sold the fagots for kindling wood to the people of the village. Sometimes she would get only a few pence each day, and sometimes a dozen or more, but on this money little Gretchen and she managed to live; they had their home, and the forest kindly furnished the wood for the fire which kept them warm in cold weather.

and placed them beside the hearth. Gretchen looked thoughtfully at them for a minute or two, and then she said, "Granny, don't you think that *somebody* in all this wide world will think of us to-night?"

"Nay, Gretchen," said Granny, "I don't think any one will."

"Well, then, Granny," said Gretchen, "the Christmas angels will, I know; so I am going to take one of your wooden shoes, and put it on the window sill outside, so that they may see it as they pass by. I am sure the stars will tell the Christmas angels where the shoe is."

"Ah, you foolish, foolish child," said Granny; "you are only getting ready for a disappointment. To-morrow morning there will be nothing whatever in the shoe. I can tell you that now."

But little Gretchen would not listen. She only shook her head and cried out: "Ah, Granny, you don't talk enough to the stars." With this she seized the shoe, and opening the door, hurried out to place it on the window-sill. It was very dark without, and something soft and cold seemed to gently kiss her hair and face. Gretchen knew by this that it was snowing, and she looked up to the sky, anxious to see if the stars were in sight, but a strong wind was tumbling the dark, heavy snow-clouds about and had shut away all else.

"Never mind," said Gretchen softly to herself, "the stars are up there, even if I can't see them, and the Christmas angels do not mind snow-storms."

Just then a rough wind went sweeping by the little girl, whispering something to her which she could not understand, and then it made a sudden rush up to the snow-clouds and parted them, so that the deep, mysterious sky appeared beyond, and shining down out of the midst of it was Gretchen's favorite star.

"Ah, little star, little star!" said the child, laughing aloud, "I knew you were there, though I couldn't see you. Will you whisper to the Christmas angels as they come by, that little Gretchen wants so very much to have a Christmas gift to-morrow morning if they have one to spare, and that she has put one of Granny's shoes upon the window-sill ready for it?"

A moment more and the little girl, standing on tiptoe, had reached the window-sill and placed the shoe upon it, and was back in the house again beside Granny and the warm fire. The two went quietly to bed, and that night as little Gretchen knelt to pray to the Heavenly Father, she thanked him for having sent the Christ Child into the world to teach all mankind how to be loving and unselfish, and in a few moments she was quietly sleeping, dreaming of the Christmas angels.

The next morning, very early, even before the sun was up, little Gretchen was awakened by the sound of sweet music coming from the village. She listened for a moment and then she knew that the choir-boys were singing the Christmas carols in the open air of the village street. She sprang out of bed and began to dress herself as quickly as possible, singing as she dressed. While Granny was slowly putting on her clothes, little Gretchen, having finished dressing herself, unfastened the door and hurried out to see what the Christmas angels had left in the old wooden shoe.

The white snow covered everything—trees, stumps, roads, and pastures—until the whole world looked like fairyland. Gretchen climbed up on a large stone which was beneath the window and carefully lifted down the wooden shoe. The snow tumbled off of it in a shower over the little girl's hands, but she did not heed that; she ran hurriedly back into the house, putting her hand into the toe of the shoe as she ran.

"Oh, Granny! Oh, Granny!" she exclaimed, "you didn't believe the Christmas angels would think about us, but see, they have, they have! Here is a dear little bird nestled down in the toe of your shoe! Oh, isn't he beautiful!"

Granny came forward and looked at what the child was holding lovingly in her hand. There she saw a tiny chick-a-dee, whose wing was evidently broken by the rough and boisterous winds of the night before, and who had taken shelter in the safe, dry toe of the old wooden shoe. She gently took the little bird out of Gretchen's hands, and skilfully bound his broken wing to his side, so that he need not hurt himself by trying to fly with it. Then she showed Gretchen how to make a nice warm nest for the little stranger, close beside the fire, and when their breakfast was ready she let Gretchen feed the little bird with a few moist crumbs.

Later in the day Gretchen carried the fresh, green boughs to the old sick man by the mill, and on her way home stopped to see and enjoy the Christmas toys of some other children whom she knew, never once wishing that they were hers. When she reached home she found that the little bird had gone to sleep. Soon, however, he opened his eyes and stretched his head up, saying just as plain as a bird could say, "Now, my new friends, I want you to give me something more to eat." Gretchen gladly fed him again, and then holding him in her lap, she softly and gently stroked his gray feathers until the little creature seemed to lose all fear of her. That evening Granny taught her a Christmas hymn and told her another beautiful Christmas story. Then Gretchen made up a funny little story to tell to the birdie. He winked his eyes and turned his head from side to side in such a droll fashion that Gretchen laughed until the tears came.

As Granny and she got ready for bed that night, Gretchen put her arms softly around Granny's neck, and whispered: "What a beautiful Christmas we have had to-day, Granny! Is there anything in the world more lovely than Christmas?"

"Nay, child, nay," said Granny, "not to such loving hearts as yours."

William Dean Howells

CHRISTMAS EVERY DAY

The little girl came into her papa's study, as she always did Saturday morning before breakfast, and asked for a story. He tried to beg off that morning, for he was very busy, but she would not let him. So he began:

“Well, once there was a little pig—”

She put her hand over his mouth and stopped him at the word. She said she had heard little pig-stories till she was perfectly sick of them.

“Well, what kind of story *shall* I tell, then?”

“About Christmas. It's getting to be the season. It's past Thanksgiving already.”

“It seems to me,” her papa argued, “that I've told as often about Christmas as I have about little pigs.”

“No difference! Christmas is more interesting.”

“Well!” Her papa roused himself from his writing by a great effort. “Well, then, I'll tell you about the little girl that wanted it Christmas every day in the year. How would you like that?”

“First-rate!” said the little girl; and she nestled into comfortable shape in his lap, ready for listening.

“Very well, then, this little pig—Oh, what are you pounding me for?”

“Because you said little pig instead of little girl.”

“I should like to know what's the difference between a little pig and a little girl that wanted it Christmas every day!”

"Papa," said the little girl, warningly, "if you don't go on, I'll *give* it to you!" And at this her papa darted off like lightning, and began to tell the story as fast as he could.

Well, once there was a little girl who liked Christmas so much that she wanted it to be Christmas every day in the year; and as soon as Thanksgiving was over she began to send postal-cards to the old Christmas Fairy to ask if she mightn't have it. But the old fairy never answered any of the postals; and after a while the little girl found out that the Fairy was pretty particular, and wouldn't notice anything but letters—not even correspondence cards in envelopes; but real letters on sheets of paper, and sealed outside with a monogram—or your initial, anyway. So, then, she began to send her letters; and in about three weeks—or just the day before Christmas, it was—she got a letter from the Fairy, saying she might have it Christmas every day for a year, and then they would see about having it longer.

The little girl was a good deal excited already, preparing for the old-fashioned, once-a-year Christmas that was coming the next day, and perhaps the Fairy's promise didn't make such an impression on her as it would have made at some other time. She just resolved to keep it to herself, and surprise everybody with it as it kept coming true; and then it slipped out of her mind altogether.

She had a splendid Christmas. She went to bed early, so as to let Santa Claus have a chance at the stockings, and in the morning she was up the first of anybody and went and felt them, and found hers all lumpy with packages of candy, and oranges and grapes, and pocket-books and rubber balls, and all kinds of small presents, and her big brother's with nothing but the tongs in them, and her young lady sister's with a new silk umbrella, and her papa's and mamma's with potatoes and pieces of coal wrapped up in tissue-paper, just as they always had every Christmas. Then she waited around till the rest of the family were up, and she was the first to burst into the library, when the doors were opened, and look at the large presents laid out on the library-table—books, and portfolios, and boxes of stationery, and breastpins, and dolls, and little stoves, and dozens of handkerchiefs, and ink-stands, and skates, and snow-shovels, and photograph-frames, and little easels, and boxes of water-colors, and Turkish paste, and nougat, and candied cherries, and dolls' houses, and waterproofs—and the big Christmas-tree, lighted and standing in a waste-basket in the middle.

She had a splendid Christmas all day. She ate so much candy that she did not want any breakfast; and the whole forenoon the presents kept pouring in that the expressman had not had time to deliver the night before; and she went round giving the presents she had got for other people, and came home and ate turkey and cranberry for dinner, and plum-pudding and nuts and raisins and oranges and more candy, and then went out and coasted, and came in with a stomach-ache, crying; and her papa said he would see if his house was turned into that sort of fool's paradise another year; and they had a light supper, and pretty early everybody went to bed cross.

Here the little girl pounded her papa in the back, again.

"Well, what now? Did I say pigs?"

"You made them *act* like pigs."

"Well, didn't they?"

"No matter; you oughtn't to put it into a story."

"Very well, then, I'll take it all out."

Her father went on:

The little girl slept very heavily, and she slept very late, but she was wakened at last by the other children dancing round her bed with their stockings full of presents in their hands.

"What is it?" said the little girl, and she rubbed her eyes and tried to rise up in bed.

"Christmas! Christmas! Christmas!" they all shouted, and waved their stockings.

"Nonsense! It was Christmas yesterday."

Her brothers and sisters just laughed. "We don't know about that. It's Christmas to-day, anyway. You come into the library and see."

Then all at once it flashed on the little girl that the Fairy was keeping her promise, and her year of Christmases was beginning. She was dreadfully sleepy, but she sprang up like a lark—a lark that had overeaten itself and gone to bed cross—and darted into the library. There it was again! Books, and portfolios, and boxes of stationery, and breastpins—

"You needn't go over it all, papa; I guess I can remember just what was there," said the little girl.

Well, and there was the Christmas-tree blazing away, and the family picking out their presents, but looking pretty sleepy, and her father perfectly puzzled, and her mother ready to cry. "I'm sure I don't see how I'm to dispose of all these things," said her mother, and her father said it seemed to him they had had something just like it the day before, but he supposed he must have dreamed it. This struck the little girl as the best kind of a joke; and so she ate so much candy she didn't want any breakfast, and went round carrying presents, and had turkey and cranberry for dinner, and then went out and coasted, and came in with a—

"Papa!"

"Well, what now?"

"What did you promise, you forgetful thing?"

"Oh! oh yes!"

"Why, that it wasn't Christmas at last, and wasn't ever going to be, any more. Now it's time for breakfast."

The little girl held her papa fast around the neck.

"You sha'n't go if you're going to leave it *so*!"

"How do you want it left?"

"Christmas once a year."

"All right," said her papa; and he went on again.

Well, there was the greatest rejoicing all over the country, and it extended clear up into Canada. The people met together everywhere, and kissed and cried for joy. The city carts went around and gathered up all the candy and raisins and nuts, and dumped them into the river; and it made the fish perfectly sick; and the whole United States, as far out as Alaska, was one blaze of bonfires, where the children were burning up their gift-books and presents of all kinds. They had the greatest *time*!

The little girl went to thank the old Fairy because she had stopped its being Christmas, and she said she hoped she would keep her promise and see that Christmas never, never came again. Then the Fairy frowned, and asked her if she was sure she knew what she meant; and the little girl asked her, Why not? and the old Fairy said that now she was behaving just as greedily as ever, and she'd better look out. This made the little girl think it all over carefully again, and she said she would be willing to have it Christmas about once in a thousand years; and then she said a hundred, and then she said ten, and at last she got down to one. Then the Fairy said that was the good old way that had pleased people ever since Christmas began, and she was agreed. Then the little girl said, "What're your shoes made of?" And the Fairy said, "Leather." And the little girl said, "Bargain's done forever," and skipped off, and hippity-hopped the whole way home, she was so glad.

"How will that do?" asked the papa.

"First-rate!" said the little girl; but she hated to have the story stop, and was rather sober. However, her mamma put her head in at the door, and asked her papa:

"Are you never coming to breakfast? What have you been telling that child?"

"Oh, just a moral tale."

The little girl caught him around the neck again.

"*We* know! Don't you tell *what*, papa! Don't you tell *what*!"

Harriet Beecher Stowe

CHRISTMAS IN POGANUC

The First Christmas.

Can any of us look back to the earlier days of our mortal pilgrimage and remember the helpless sense of desolation and loneliness caused by being forced to go off to the stillness and darkness of a solitary bed far from all the beloved voices and employments and sights of life? Can we remember lying, hearing distant voices, and laughs of more fortunate, older people and the opening and shutting of distant doors, that told of scenes of animation and interest from which we were excluded? How doleful sounded the tick of the clock, and how dismal was the darkness as sunshine faded from the window, leaving only a square of dusky dimness in place of daylight!

All who remember these will sympathize with Dolly, who was hustled off to bed by Nabby the minute supper was over, that she might have the decks clear for action.

"Now be a good girl; shut your eyes, and say your prayers, and go right to sleep," had been Nabby's parting injunction as she went out, closing the door after her.

The little head sunk into the pillow, and Dolly recited her usual liturgy of "Our Father who art in heaven," and "I pray God to bless my dear father and mother and all my dear friends and relations, and make me a good girl," and ending with

"'Now I lay me down to sleep.'"

But sleep she could not. The wide, bright, wistful blue eyes lay shining like two stars toward the fading light in the window, and the little ears were strained to catch every sound. She heard the shouts of Tom and Bill and the loud barking of Spring as they swept out of the door; and the sound went to her heart. Spring—her faithful attendant, the most loving and sympathetic of dogs, her friend and confidential counselor in many a solitary ramble—Spring had gone with the boys to see the sight, and left her alone. She began to pity herself and cry softly on her pillow. For a while she could hear Nabby's energetic movements below, washing up dishes, putting back chairs, and giving energetic thumps and bangs here and there, as her way was of producing order. But by and by that was all over, and she heard the loud shutting of the kitchen door and Nabby's voice chatting with her attendant as she went off to the scene of gaiety.

In those simple, innocent days in New England villages nobody thought of locking house doors at night. There was in those times no idea either of tramps or burglars, and many a night in summer had Dolly lain awake and heard the voices of tree-toads and whip-poor-wills mingling with the whisper of leaves and the swaying of elm boughs, while the great outside door of the house lay broad open in the moonlight. But then this was when everybody was in the house and asleep, when the door of her parents' room stood open on the front hall, and she knew she could run to the paternal bed in a minute for protection. Now, however, she knew the house was empty. Everybody had gone out of it; and there is something fearful to a little lonely body in the possibilities of a great, empty house. She got up and opened her door, and the "tick-tock" of the old kitchen clock for a moment seemed like company; but pretty soon its ticking began to strike louder and louder with a nervous insistency on her ear, till the nerves quivered and vibrated, and she couldn't go to sleep. She lay and listened to all the noises outside. It was a still, clear, freezing night, when the least sound clinked with a metallic resonance. She heard the runners of sleighs squeaking and crunching over the frozen road, and the lively jingle of bells. They would come nearer, nearer, pass by the house, and go off in the distance. Those were the happy folks going to see the gold star and the

Christmas greens in the church. The gold star, the Christmas greens, had all the more attraction from their vagueness. Dolly was a fanciful little creature, and the clear air and romantic scenery of a mountain town had fed her imagination. Stories she had never read, except in the Bible and the Pilgrim's Progress, but her very soul had vibrated with the descriptions of the celestial city—something vague, bright, glorious, lying beyond some dark river; and Nabby's rude account of what was going on in the church suggested those images.

Finally a bright thought popped into her little head. She could see the church from the front windows of the house; she would go there and look. In haste she sprang out of bed and dressed herself. It was sharp and freezing in the fireless chamber, but Dolly's blood had a racing, healthy tingle to it; she didn't mind cold. She wrapped her cloak around her and tied on her hood and ran to the front windows. There it was, to be sure—the little church with its sharp-pointed windows, every pane of which was sending streams of light across the glittering snow. There was a crowd around the door, and men and boys looking in at the windows. Dolly's soul was fired. But the elm boughs a little obstructed her vision; she thought she would go down and look at it from the yard. So down-stairs she ran, but as she opened the door the sound of the chant rolled out into the darkness with sweet and solemn cadence:

"*Glory be to God on high; and on earth peace, good will toward men.*"

Dolly's soul was all aglow—her nerves tingled and vibrated; she thought of the bells ringing in the celestial city; she could no longer contain herself, but faster and faster the little hooded form scudded across the snowy plain and pushed in among the dark cluster of spectators at the door. All made way for the child, and in a moment, whether in the body or out she could not tell, Dolly was sitting in a little nook under a bower of spruce, gazing at the star and listening to the voices:

"We praise Thee, we bless Thee, we worship Thee, we glorify Thee, we give thanks to Thee for Thy great glory, O Lord God, Heavenly King, God, the Father Almighty."

Her heart throbbed and beat; she trembled with a strange happiness and sat as one entranced till the music was over. Then came reading, the rustle and murmur of people kneeling, and then they all rose and there was the solemn buzz of voices repeating the Creed with a curious lulling sound to her ear. There was old Mr. Danforth with his spectacles on, reading with a pompous tone, as if to witness a good confession for the church; and there were Squire Lewis and old Ma'am Lewis; and there was one place where they all bowed their heads and all the ladies made courtesies—all of which entertained her mightily.

When the sermon began Dolly got fast asleep, and slept as quietly as a pet lamb in a meadow, lying in a little warm roll back under the shadows of the spruces. She was so tired and so sound asleep that she did not wake when the service ended, lying serenely curled up, and having perhaps pleasant dreams. She might have had the fortunes of little Goody Two-Shoes, whose history was detailed in one of the few children's books then printed, had not two friends united to find her out.

Spring, who had got into the slip with the boys, and been an equally attentive and edified listener, after service began a tour of investigation, dog-fashion, with his nose; for how could a minister's dog form a suitable judgment of any new procedure if he was repressed from the use of his own leading faculty? So, Spring went round the church conscientiously, smelling at pew doors, smelling of the greens, smelling at the heels of gentlemen and ladies, till he came near the door of the church, when he suddenly smelt something which called for immediate attention, and he made a side dart into the thicket where Dolly was sleeping, and began licking her face and hands and pulling her dress, giving short barks occasionally, as if to say, "Come, Dolly, wake up!" At the same instant Hiel, who had seen her from the gallery, came down just as the little one was sitting up with a dazed, bewildered air.

"Why, Dolly, how came you out o' bed this time o' night? Don't ye know the nine o'clock bell's jest rung?"

Dolly knew Hiel well enough—what child in the village did not? She reached up her little hands, saying in an apologetic fashion:

"They were all gone away, and I was so lonesome!"

Hiel took her up in his long arms and carried her home, and was just entering the house door with her as the sleigh drove up with Parson Cushing and his wife.

"Wal, Parson, your folks has all ben to the 'lumination—Nabby and Bill and Tom and Dolly here; found her all rolled up in a heap like a rabbit under the cedars."

"Why, Dolly Cushing!" exclaimed her mother. "What upon earth got you out of bed this time of night? You'll catch your death o' cold."

"I was all alone," said Dolly, with a piteous bleat.

"Oh, there, there, wife; don't say a word," put in the parson. "Get her off to bed. Never mind, Dolly, don't you cry;" for Parson Cushing was a soft-hearted gentleman and couldn't bear the sight of Dolly's quivering under lip. So Dolly told her little story, how she had been promised a sugar dog by Nabby if she'd be a good girl and go to sleep, and how she couldn't go to sleep, and how she just went down to look from the yard, and how the music drew her right over.

"There, there," said Parson Cushing, "go to bed, Dolly; and if Nabby don't give you a sugar dog, I will. This Christmas dressing is all nonsense," he added, "but the child's not to blame—it was natural."

"After all," he said to his wife the last thing after they were settled for the night, "our little Dolly is an unusual child. There were not many little girls that would have dared to do that. I shall preach a sermon right away that will set all this Christmas matter straight," said the Doctor. "There is not a shadow of evidence that the first Christians kept Christmas. It wasn't kept for the first three centuries, nor was Christ born anywhere near the 25th of December."

*   *   *   *   *

The next morning found little Dolly's blue eyes wide open with all the wondering eagerness of a new idea.

Dolly had her wise thoughts about Christmas. She had been terribly frightened at first, when she was brought home from the church; but when her papa kissed her and promised her a sugar dog she was quite sure that, whatever the unexplained mystery might be, he did not think the lovely scene of the night before a wicked one. And when Mrs. Cushing came and covered the little girl up warmly in bed, she only said to her, "Dolly, you must never get out of bed again at night after you are put there; you might have caught a dreadful cold and been sick and died, and then we should have lost our little Dolly." So Dolly promised quite readily to be good and lie still ever after, no matter what attractions might be on foot in the community.

Much was gained, however, and it was all clear gain; and forthwith the little fanciful head proceeded to make the most of it, thinking over every feature of the wonder. The child had a vibrating, musical organization, and the sway and rush of the chanting still sounded in her ears and reminded her of that wonderful story in the "Pilgrim's Progress", where the gate of the celestial city swung open, and there were voices that sung, "Blessing and honor and glory and power be unto Him who sitteth on the throne." And then that wonderful star, that shone just as if it were a real star—how could it be! For Miss Ida Lewis, being a young lady of native artistic genius, had cut a little hole in the centre of her gilt paper star, behind which was placed a candle, so that it gave real light, in a way most astonishing to untaught eyes. In Dolly's simple view it verged on the supernatural—perhaps it was *the* very real star read about in the Gospel story. Why not? Dolly was at the happy age when anything bright and heavenly seemed credible, and had the child-faith to which all things were possible.

"I wish, my dear," said Mrs. Cushing, after they were retired to their room for the night, "that to-morrow morning you would read the account of the birth of Christ in St. Matthew, and give the children some advice upon the proper way of keeping Christmas."

"Well, but you know we don't *keep* Christmas; nobody knows anything about Christmas," said the Doctor.

"You know what I mean, my dear," replied his wife. "You know that my mother and her family *do* keep Christmas. I always heard of it when I was a child; and even now, though I have been out of the way of it so long, I cannot help a sort of kindly feeling toward these ways. I am not surprised at all that the children got drawn over last night to the service. I think it's the most natural thing in the world, and I know by experience just how attractive such things are. I shouldn't wonder if this other church should draw very seriously on your congregation; but I don't want it to begin by taking away our own children. Dolly is an inquisitive child; a child that thinks a good deal, and she'll be asking all sorts of questions about the why and wherefore of what she saw last night."

"Oh, yes, Dolly is a bright one. Dolly's an uncommon child," said the Doctor, who had a pardonable pride in his children—they being, in fact, the only worldly treasure that he was at all rich in.

He rose up early on the following Sabbath and proceeded to buy a sugar dog at the store of Lucius Jenks, and when Dolly came down to breakfast he called her to him and presented it, saying as he kissed her:

"Papa gives you this, not because it is Christmas, but because he loves his little Dolly."

"But *isn't* it Christmas?" asked Dolly with a puzzled air.

"No, child; nobody knows when Christ was born, and there is nothing in the Bible to tell us *when* to keep Christmas."

And then in family worship the Doctor read the account of the birth of Christ and of the shepherds abiding in the fields who came at the call of the angels, and they sung the old hymn:

"While shepherds watched their flocks by night."

"Now, children," he said when all was over, "you must be good children and go to school. If we are going to keep any day on account of the birth of Christ, the best way to keep it is by doing all our duties on that day better than any other. Your duty is to be good children, go to school and mind your lessons."

Tom and Bill were quite ready to fall in with their father's view of the matter. As for Dolly, she put her little tongue advisedly to the back of her sugar dog and found that he was very sweet indeed—a most tempting little animal. She even went so far as to nibble off a bit of the green ground he stood on—yet resolved heroically not to eat him at once, but to make him last as long as possible. She wrapped him tenderly in cotton and took him to the school with her, and when her confidential friend, Bessie Lewis, displayed her Christmas gifts, Dolly had something on her side to show, though she shook her curly head and informed Bessie in strict confidence that there wasn't any such thing as Christmas, her papa had told her so—a heresy which Bessie forthwith reported when she went home at noon.

"Poor little child—and did she say so?" asked gentle old Grandmamma Lewis. "Well, dear, you mustn't blame her—she don't know any better. You bring the little one in here to-night and I'll give her a Christmas cooky. I'm sorry for such children."

And so, after school, Dolly went in to see dear old Madam Lewis, who sat in her rocking-chair in the front parlor, where the fire was snapping behind great tall brass andirons and all the pictures were overshadowed with boughs of spruce and pine. Dolly gazed about her with awe and wonder. Over one of the pictures was suspended a cross of green with flowers of white everlasting.

"What is *that* for?" asked Dolly, pointing solemnly with her little forefinger, and speaking under her breath.

"Dear child, that is the picture of my poor boy who died—ever so many years ago. That is my cross—we have all one—to carry."

Dolly did not half understand these words, but she saw tears in the gentle old lady's eyes and was afraid to ask more.

She accepted thankfully and with her nicest and best executed courtesy a Christmas cooky representing a good-sized fish, with fins all spread and pink sugar-plums for eyes, and went home marveling yet more about this mystery of Christmas.

As she was crossing the green to go home the Poganuc stage drove in, with Hiel seated on high, whipping up his horses to make them execute that grand *entrée* which was the glory of his daily existence.

Now that the stage was on runners, and slipped noiselessly over the smooth frozen plain, Hiel cracked his whip more energetically and shouted louder, first to one horse then to another, to make up for the loss of the rattling wheels; and he generally had the satisfaction of seeing all the women rushing distractedly to doors and windows, and imagined them saying, "There's Hiel; the stage is in!"

"Hulloa, Dolly!" he called out, drawing up with a suddenness which threw the fore-horses back upon their haunches. "I've got a bundle for your folks. Want to ride? You may jest jump up here by me and I'll take you 'round to your father's door;" and so Dolly reached up her little red-mittened hand, and Hiel drew her up beside him.

"'Xpect ye want a bit of a ride, and I've got a bundle for Widder Badger, down on South Street, so I guess I'll go 'round that way to make it longer. I 'xpect this 'ere bundle is from some of your ma's folks in Boston—'Piscopals they be and keeps Christmas. Good-sized bundle 'tis; reckon it'll come handy in a good many ways."

So, after finishing his detour, Hiel landed his little charge at the parsonage door.

"Reckon I'll be over when I've put up my hosses," he said to Nabby when he handed down the bundle to her. "I hain't been to see you much lately, Nabby, and I know you've been a-pinin' after me, but fact is—"

"Well, now, Hiel Jones, you jest shet up with your imperence," said Nabby, with flashing eyes; "you jest look out or you'll get suthin."

"I 'xpect to get a kiss when I come 'round to-night," said Hiel, composedly. "Take care o' that air bundle, now; mebbe there's glass or crockery in't."

"Hiel Jones," said Nabby, "don't give me none o' your saace, for I won't take it. Jim Sawin said last night you was the brassiest man he ever see. He said there was brass enough in your face to make a kettle of."

"You tell him there's sap enough in his head to fill it, anyway," said Hiel. "Good bye, Nabby, I'll come 'round this evenin'," and he drove away at a rattling pace, while Nabby, with flushed cheeks and snapping eyes, soliloquized:

"Well, I hope he will come! I'd jest like a chance to show him how little I care for him."

Meanwhile the bundle was soon opened, and contained a store of treasures: a smart little red dress and a pair of red shoes for Dolly, a half dozen pocket-handkerchiefs for Dr. Cushing, and "Robinson Crusoe" and "Sanford and Merton," handsomely bound, for the boys, and a bonnet trimming for Mrs. Cushing. These were accompanied by a characteristic letter from Aunt Debby Kittery, opening as follows:

> "Dear Sister:
>
> "Mother worries because she thinks you won't get any Christmas presents. However, this comes to give every one of you some of the crumbs which fall from the church's table, and Mother says she wishes you all a pious Christmas, which she thinks is better than a merry one. If I didn't lay violent hands on her she would use all our substance in riotous giving of Christmas presents to all the beggars and chimney sweeps in Boston. She is in good health and talks daily of wanting to see you and the children; and I hope before long you will bring some of them, and come and make us a visit.
>
> "Your affectionate sister,
>
> "Debby Kittery."

There was a scene of exultation and clamor in the parsonage as these presents were pulled out and discussed; and when all possible joy was procured from them in the sitting-room, the children rushed in a body into the kitchen and showed them to Nabby, calling on her to join their acclamations.

On the whole, when Dolly had said her prayers that night and thought the matter over, she concluded that her Christmas Day had been quite a success.

The Second Christmas.

Once more had Christmas come round in Poganuc; once more the Episcopal church was being dressed with ground-pine and spruce; but this year economy had begun to make its claims felt. An illumination might do very well to open a church, but there were many who said "to what purpose is this waste?" when the proposition was made to renew it yearly. Consequently it was resolved to hold the Christmas Eve service with only that necessary amount of light which would enable the worshipers to read the prayers.

On this Christmas Eve Dolly went to bed at her usual hour with a resigned and quiet spirit. She felt herself a year older, and more than a year wiser, than when Christmas had first dawned upon her consciousness.

Mis' Persis appeared on the ground by day-dawn. A great kettle was slung over the kitchen fire, in which cakes of tallow were speedily liquefying; a frame was placed quite across the kitchen to sustain candle-rods, with a train of boards underneath to catch the drippings, and Mis' Persis, with a brow like one of the Fates, announced: "Now we can't hev any young 'uns in this kitchen to-day;" and Dolly saw that there was no getting any attention in that quarter.

Mis' Persis, in a gracious Saturday afternoon mood, sitting in her own tent-door dispensing hospitalities and cookies, was one thing; but Mis' Persis in her armor, with her loins girded and a hard day's work to be conquered, was quite another: she was terrible as Minerva with her helmet on.

Dinner-baskets for all the children were hastily packed, and they were sent off to school with the injunction on no account to show their faces about the premises till night. The Doctor, warned of what was going on, retreated to his study at the top of the house, where, serenely above the lower cares of earth, he sailed off into President Edwards' treatise on the nature of true virtue, concerning which he was preparing a paper to read at the next association meeting.

That candles were a necessity of life he was well convinced, and by faith he dimly accepted the fact that one day in the year the whole house was to be devoted and given up to this manufacture; and his part of the business, as he understood it, was, clearly, to keep himself out of the way till it was over.

"There won't be much of a dinner at home, anyway," said Nabby to Dolly, as she packed her basket with an extra doughnut or two. "I've got to go to church to-day, 'cause I'm one of the singers, and your ma'll be busy waitin' on *her*; so we shall just have a pick-up dinner, and you be sure not to come home till night; by that time it'll be all over."

Dolly trotted off to school well content with the prospect before her: a nooning, with leave to play with the girls at school, was not an unpleasant idea.

But the first thing that saluted her on her arrival was that Bessie Lewis—her own dear, particular Bessie—was going to have a Christmas party at her house that afternoon, and was around distributing invitations right and left among the scholars with a generous freedom.

"We are going to have nuts, and raisins, and cakes, and mottoes," said Bessie, with artless triumph. The news of this bill of fare spread like wildfire through the school.

Never had a party been heard of which contemplated such a liberal entertainment, for the rising generation of Poganuc were by no means wearied with indulgence, and raisins and almonds stood for grandeur with them. But these *mottoes*, which consisted of bits of confectionery wrapped up in printed couplets of sentimental poetry, were an unheard-of refinement. Bessie assured them that her papa had sent clear to Boston for them, and whoever got one would have his or her fortune told by it.

The school was a small, select one, comprising the children of all ages from the best families of Poganuc. Both boys and girls, and all with great impartiality, had been invited. Miss Titcome, the teacher, quite readily promised to dismiss at three o'clock that afternoon any scholar who should bring a permission from parents, and the children nothing doubted that such a permission was obtainable.

Dolly alone saw a cloud in the horizon. She had been sent away with strict injunctions not to return till evening, and children in those days never presumed to make any exceptions in obeying an absolute command of their parents.

"But, of course, you will go home at noon and ask your mother, and of course she'll let you; won't she, girls?" said Bessie.

"Oh, certainly; of course she will," said all the older girls, "because you know a party is a thing that don't happen every day, and your mother would think it strange if you *didn't* come and ask her." So, too, thought Miss Titcome, a most exemplary, precise and proper young lady, who always moved and spoke and thought as became a schoolmistress, so that, although she was in reality only twenty years old, Dolly considered her as a very advanced and ancient person—if anything, a little older than her father and mother.

Even she was of opinion that Dolly might properly go home to lay a case of such importance before her mother; and so Dolly rushed home after the morning school was over, running with all her might, and increasing in mental excitement as she ran. Her bonnet blew off upon her shoulders, her curls flew behind her in the wind, and she most inconsiderately used up the little stock of breath that she would want to set her cause in order before her mother.

Just here we must beg any mother and housekeeper to imagine herself in the very midst of the most delicate, perplexing and laborious of household tasks, when interruption is most irksome and perilous, suddenly called to discuss with a child some new and startling proposition to which at the moment she cannot even give a thought.

Mrs. Cushing was sitting in the kitchen with Mis' Persis, by the side of a caldron of melted tallow, kept in a fluid state by the heat of a portable furnace on which it stood. A long train of half-dipped candles hung like so many stalactites from the frames on which the rods rested, and the two were patiently dipping set after set and replacing them again on the frame.

"As sure as I'm alive! if there isn't Dolly Cushing comin' back—runnin' and tearin' like a wild cretur'," said Mis' Persis. "She'll be in here in a minute and knock everything down!"

Mrs. Cushing looked, and with a quick movement stepped to the door.

"Dolly! what are you here for? Didn't I tell you not to come home this noon?"

"Oh, mamma, there's going to be a party at General Lewis'—Bessie's party—and the girls are all going; mayn't I go?"

"No, you can't; it's impossible," said her mother. "Your best dress isn't ready to wear, and there's nobody can spend time to get you ready. Go right back to school."

"But, mamma—"

"Go!" said her mother, in the decisive tone that mothers used in the old days, when arguing with children was not a possibility.

"What's all this about?" asked the Doctor, looking out of the door.

"Why," said Mrs. Cushing, "there's going to be a party at General Lewis', and Dolly is wild to go. It's just impossible for me to attend to her now."

"Oh, I don't want her intimate at Lewis's," said the Doctor, and immediately he came out behind his wife.

"There; run away to school, Dolly," he said. "Don't trouble your mother; you don't want to go to parties; why, it's foolish to think of it. Run away now, and don't think any more about it—there's a good girl!"

Dolly turned and went back to school, the tears freezing on her cheek as she went. As for not thinking any more about it—that was impossible.

When three o'clock came, scholar after scholar rose and departed, until at last Dolly was the only one remaining in the school-room.

When Dolly came home that night the coast was clear, and the candles were finished and put away to harden in a freezing cold room; the kitchen was once more restored, and Nabby bustled about getting supper as if nothing had happened.

"I really feel sorry about poor little Dolly," said Mrs. Cushing to her husband.

"Do you think she cared much?" asked the Doctor, looking as if a new possibility had struck his mind.

"Yes, indeed, poor child, she went away crying; but what could I do about it? I couldn't stop to dress her."

"Wife, we must take her somewhere to make up for it," said the Doctor.

Just then the stage stopped at the door and a bundle from Boston was handed in. Dolly's tears were soon wiped and dried, and her mourning was turned into joy when a large jointed London doll emerged from the bundle, the Christmas gift of her grandmother in Boston.

Dolly's former darling was old and shabby, but this was of twice the size, and with cheeks exhibiting a state of the most florid health.

Besides this there was, as usual in grandmamma's Christmas bundle, something for every member of the family; and so the evening went on festive wings.

Poor little Dolly! only that afternoon she had watered with her tears, at school, the dismal long straight seam, which stretched on before her as life sometimes does to us, bare, disagreeable and cheerless. She had come home crying, little dreaming of the joy just approaching; but before bed-time no cricket in the hearth was cheerier or more noisy. She took the new dolly to bed with her, and could hardly sleep, for the excitement of her company.

Meanwhile, Hiel had brought the Doctor a message to the following effect:

"I was drivin' by Tim Hawkins', and Mis' Hawkins she comes out and says they're goin' to hev an apple-cuttin' there to-morrow night, and she would like to hev you and Mis' Cushin' and all your folks come—Nabby and all."

The Doctor and his lady of course assented.

"Wal, then, Doctor—ef it's all one to you," continued Hiel, "I'd like to take ye over in my new double sleigh. I've jest got two new strings o' bells up from Boston, and I think we'll sort o' make the snow fly. S'pose there'd be no objections to takin' my mother 'long with ye?"

"Oh, Hiel, we shall be delighted to go in company with your mother, and we're ever so much obliged to you," said Mrs. Cushing.

"Wal, I'll be round by six o'clock," said Hiel.

"Then, wife," said the Doctor, "we'll take Dolly, and make up for the loss of her party."

Punctually at six, Hiel's two horses, with all their bells jingling, stood at the door of the parsonage, whence Tom and Bill, who had been waiting with caps and mittens on for the last half hour, burst forth with irrepressible shouts of welcome.

"Take care now, boys; don't haul them buffalo skins out on t' the snow," said Hiel. "Don't get things in a muss gen'ally; wait for your ma and the Doctor. Got to stow the grown folks in fust; boys kin hang on anywhere."

And so first came Mrs. Cushing and the Doctor, and were installed on the back seat, with Dolly in between. Then hot bricks were handed in to keep feet warm, and the buffalo robe was tucked down securely. Then Nabby took her seat by Hiel in front, and the sleigh drove round for old Mrs. Jones. The Doctor insisted on giving up his place to her and tucking her warmly under the buffalo robe, while he took the middle seat and acted as moderator between the boys, who were in a wild state of hilarity. Spring, with explosive barks, raced first on this and then on that side of the sleigh as it flew swiftly over the smooth frozen road.

The stars blinked white and clear out of a deep blue sky, and the path wound up-hill among cedars and junipers and clumps of mountain laurel, on whose broad green leaves the tufts of snow lay like clusters of white roses. The keen clear air was full of stimulus and vigor; and so Hiel's proposition to take the longest way met with enthusiastic welcome from all the party. Next to being a bird, and having wings, is the sensation of being borne over the snow by a pair of spirited horses who enjoy the race, apparently, as much as those they draw. Though Hiel contrived to make the ride about eight miles, it yet seemed but a short time before the party drove up to the great red farmhouse, whose lighted windows sent streams of radiant welcome far out into the night.

Our little Dolly had had an evening of unmixed bliss. Everybody had petted her, and talked to her, and been delighted with her sayings and doings, and she was carrying home a paper parcel of sweet things which good Mrs. Hawkins had forced into her hand at parting. She had spent a really happy Christmas!

Clement Clarke Moore

Twas the Night before Christmas: A Visit from St. Nicholas

INTRODUCTION

A mid the many celebrations last Christmas Eve, in various places by different persons, there was one, in New York City, not like any other anywhere. A company of men, women, and children went together just after the evening service in their church, and, standing around the tomb of the author of "A Visit from St. Nicholas," recited together the words of the poem which we all know so well and love so dearly.

Dr. Clement C. Moore, who wrote the poem, never expected that he would be remembered by it. If he expected to be famous at all as a writer, he thought it would be because of the Hebrew Dictionary that he wrote.

He was born in a house near Chelsea Square, New York City, in 1781; and he lived there all his life. It was a great big house, with fireplaces in it;—just the house to be living in on Christmas Eve.

Dr. Moore had children. He liked writing poetry for them even more than he liked writing a Hebrew Dictionary. He wrote a whole book of poems for them.

One year he wrote this poem, which we usually call "'Twas the Night before Christmas," to give to his children for a Christmas present. They read it just after they had hung up their stockings before one of the big fireplaces in their house. Afterward, they learned it, and sometimes recited it, just as other children learn it and recite it now.

It was printed in a newspaper. Then a magazine printed it, and after a time it was printed in the school readers. Later it was printed by itself, with pictures. Then it was translated into German, French, and many other languages. It was even made into "Braille"; which is the raised printing that blind children read with their fingers. But never has it been given to us in so attractive a form as in this book. It has happened that almost all the children in the world know this poem. How few of them know any Hebrew!

Every Christmas Eve the young men studying to be ministers at the General Theological Seminary, New York City, put a holly wreath around Dr. Moore's picture, which is on the wall of their dining-room. Why? Because he gave the ground on which the General Theological Seminary stands? Because he wrote a Hebrew Dictionary? No. They do it because he was the author of "A Visit from St. Nicholas."

Most of the children probably know the words of the poem. They are old. But the pictures that Miss Jessie Willcox Smith has painted for this edition of it are new. All the children, probably, have seen other pictures painted by Miss Smith, showing children at other seasons of the year. How much they will enjoy looking at these pictures, showing children on that night that all children like best,—Christmas Eve!

E. McC.

T was the night before Christmas, when all through the house
Not a creature was stirring, not even a mouse;
The stockings were hung by the chimney with care
In hopes that St. Nicholas soon would be there;

The children were nestled all snug in their beds,
While visions of sugar-plums danced in their heads;
And mamma in her kerchief, and I in my cap,
Had just settled our brains for a long winter's nap,

When out on the lawn there arose such a clatter,
I sprang from the bed to see what was the matter.
Away to the window I flew like a flash,
Tore open the shutters and threw up the sash.

The moon on the breast of the new-fallen snow
Gave the lustre of mid-day to objects below,
When, what to my wondering eyes should appear,
But a miniature sleigh, and eight tiny reindeer,

With a little old driver, so lively and quick,
I knew in a moment it must be St. Nick.

More rapid than eagles his coursers they came,
And he whistled, and shouted, and called them by name:

Now, **Dasher!** now, **Dancer!** now, **Prancer** and **Vixen!**
On, **Comet!** on, **Cupid!** on, **Donder** and **Blitzen!**
To the top of the porch! to the top of the wall!
Now dash away! dash away! dash away all!"

As dry leaves that before the wild hurricane fly,
When they meet with an obstacle, mount to the sky;
So up to the house-top the coursers they flew,
With the sleigh full of Toys, and St. Nicholas too.

And then, in a twinkling, I heard on the roof
The prancing and pawing of each little hoof.
As I drew in my head, and was turning around,
Down the chimney St. Nicholas came with a bound.

He was dressed all in fur, from his head to his foot,
And his clothes were all tarnished with ashes and soot;
A bundle of Toys he had flung on his back,
And he looked like a peddler just opening his pack.

His eyes—how they twinkled! his dimples how merry!
His cheeks were like roses, his nose like a cherry!
His droll little mouth was drawn up like a bow,
And the beard of his chin was as white as the snow;

The stump of a pipe he held tight in his teeth,
And the smoke it encircled his head like a wreath;
He had a broad face and a little round belly,

That shook when he laughed, like a bowlful of jelly.

He was chubby and plump, a right jolly old elf,
And I laughed when I saw him, in spite of myself;
A wink of his eye and a twist of his head,
Soon gave me to know I had nothing to dread;

He spoke not a word, but went straight to his work,
And filled all the stockings; then turned with a jerk,
And laying his finger aside of his nose,
And giving a nod, up the chimney he rose;

He sprang to his sleigh, to his team gave a whistle,
And away they all flew like the down of a thistle.
But I heard him exclaim, ere he drove out of sight,
"Happy Christmas to all, and to all a good-night."

Charles Dickens

A Christmas Tree

I have been looking on, this evening, at a merry company of children assembled round that pretty German toy, a Christmas Tree. The tree was planted in the middle of a great round table, and towered high above their heads. It was brilliantly lighted by a multitude of little tapers; and everywhere sparkled and glittered with bright objects. There were rosy-cheeked dolls, hiding behind the green leaves; and there were real watches (with movable hands, at least, and an endless capacity of being wound up) dangling from innumerable twigs; there were French-polished tables, chairs, bedsteads, wardrobes, eight-day clocks, and various other articles of domestic furniture (wonderfully made, in tin, at Wolverhampton), perched among the boughs, as if in preparation for some fairy housekeeping; there were jolly, broad-faced little men, much more agreeable in appearance than many real men—and no wonder, for their heads took off, and showed them to be full of sugar-plums; there were fiddles and drums; there were tambourines, books, work-boxes, paint-boxes, sweetmeat-boxes, peep-show boxes, and all kinds of boxes; there were trinkets for the elder girls, far brighter than any grown-up gold and jewels; there were baskets and pincushions in all devices; there were guns, swords, and banners; there were witches standing in enchanted rings of pasteboard, to tell fortunes; there were teetotums, humming-tops, needle-cases, pen-wipers, smelling-bottles, conversation-cards, bouquet-holders; real fruit, made artificially dazzling with gold leaf; imitation apples, pears, and walnuts, crammed with surprises; in short, as a pretty child, before me, delightedly whispered to another pretty child, her bosom friend, "There was everything, and more." This motley collection of odd objects, clustering on the tree like magic fruit, and flashing back the bright looks directed towards it from every side—some of the diamond-eyes admiring it were hardly on a level with the table, and a few were languishing in timid wonder on the bosoms of pretty mothers, aunts, and nurses—made a lively realisation of the fancies of childhood; and set me thinking how all the trees that grow and all the things that come into existence on the earth, have their wild adornments at that well-remembered time.

Being now at home again, and alone, the only person in the house awake, my thoughts are drawn back, by a fascination which I do not care to resist, to my own childhood. I begin to consider, what do we all remember best upon the branches of the Christmas Tree of our own young Christmas days, by which we climbed to real life.

Straight, in the middle of the room, cramped in the freedom of its growth by no encircling walls or soon-reached ceiling, a shadowy tree arises; and, looking up into the dreamy brightness of its top—for I observe in this tree the singular property that it appears to grow downward towards the earth—I look into my youngest Christmas recollections!

All toys at first, I find. Up yonder, among the green holly and red berries, is the Tumbler with his hands in his pockets, who wouldn't lie down, but whenever he was put upon the floor, persisted in rolling his fat body about, until he rolled himself still, and brought those lobster eyes of his to bear upon me—when I affected to laugh very much, but in my heart of hearts was extremely doubtful of him. Close beside him is that infernal snuff-box, out of which there sprang a demoniacal Counsellor in a black gown, with an obnoxious head of hair, and a red cloth mouth, wide open, who was not to be endured on any terms, but could not be put away either; for he used suddenly, in a highly magnified state, to fly out of Mammoth Snuff-boxes in dreams, when least expected. Nor is the frog with cobbler's wax on his tail, far off; for there was no knowing where he wouldn't jump; and when he flew over the candle, and came upon one's hand with that spotted back—red on a green ground—he was horrible. The cardboard lady in a blue-silk skirt, who was stood up against the candlestick to dance, and whom I see on the same branch, was milder, and was beautiful; but I can't say as much for the larger cardboard man, who used to be hung against the wall and pulled by a string; there was a sinister expression in that nose of his; and when he got his legs round his neck (which he very often did), he was ghastly, and not a creature to be alone with.

When did that dreadful Mask first look at me? Who put it on, and why was I so frightened that the sight of it is an era in my life? It is not a hideous visage in itself; it is even meant to be droll, why then were its stolid features so intolerable? Surely not because it hid the wearer's face. An apron would have done as much; and though I should have preferred even the apron away, it would not have been absolutely insupportable, like the mask. Was it the immovability of the mask? The doll's face was immovable, but I was not afraid of *her*. Perhaps that fixed and set change coming over a real face, infused into my quickened heart some remote suggestion and dread of the universal change that is to come on every face, and make it still? Nothing reconciled me to it. No drummers, from whom proceeded a melancholy chirping on the turning of a handle; no regiment of soldiers, with a mute band, taken out of a box, and fitted, one by one, upon a stiff and lazy little set of lazy-tongs; no old woman, made of wires and a brown-paper composition, cutting up a pie for two small children; could give me a permanent comfort, for a long time. Nor was it any satisfaction to be shown the Mask, and see that it was made of paper, or to have it locked up and be assured that no one wore it. The mere recollection of that fixed face, the mere knowledge of its existence anywhere, was sufficient to awake me in the night all perspiration and horror, with, "O I know it's coming! O the mask!"

I never wondered what the dear old donkey with the panniers—there he is! was made of, then! His hide was real to the touch, I recollect. And the great black horse with the round red spots all over him—the horse that I could even get upon—I never wondered what had brought him to that strange condition, or thought that such a horse was not commonly seen at Newmarket. The four horses of no colour, next to him, that went into the waggon of cheeses, and could be taken out and stabled under the piano, appear to have bits of fur-tippet for their tails, and other bits for their manes, and to stand on pegs instead of legs, but it was not so when they were brought home for a Christmas present. They were all right, then; neither was their harness unceremoniously nailed into their chests, as appears to be the case now. The tinkling works of the music-cart, I *did* find out, to be made of quill tooth-picks and wire; and I always thought that little tumbler in his shirt sleeves, perpetually swarming up one side of a wooden frame, and coming down, head foremost, on the other, rather a weak-minded person—though good-natured; but the Jacob's Ladder, next him, made of little squares of red wood, that went flapping and clattering over one another, each developing a different picture, and the whole enlivened by small bells, was a mighty marvel and a great delight.

Ah! The Doll's house!—of which I was not proprietor, but where I visited. I don't admire the Houses of Parliament half so much as that stone-fronted mansion with real glass windows, and door-steps, and a real balcony—greener than I ever see now, except at watering places; and even they afford but a poor imitation. And though it *did* open all at once, the entire house-front (which was a blow, I admit, as cancelling the fiction of a staircase), it was but to shut it up again, and I could believe. Even open, there were three distinct rooms in it: a sitting-room and bed-room, elegantly furnished, and best of all, a kitchen, with uncommonly soft fire-irons, a plentiful assortment of diminutive utensils—oh, the warming-pan!—and a tin man-cook in profile, who was always going to fry two fish. What Barmecide justice have I done to the noble feasts wherein the set of wooden platters figured, each with its own peculiar delicacy, as a ham or turkey, glued tight on to it, and garnished with something green, which I recollect as moss! Could all the Temperance Societies of these later days, united, give me such a tea-drinking as I have had through the means of yonder little set of blue crockery, which really would hold liquid (it ran out of the small wooden cask, I recollect, and tasted of matches), and which made tea, nectar. And if the two legs of the ineffectual little sugar-tongs did tumble over one another, and want purpose, like Punch's hands, what does it matter? And if I did once shriek out, as a poisoned child, and strike the fashionable company with consternation, by reason of having drunk a little teaspoon, inadvertently dissolved in too hot tea, I was never the worse for it, except by a powder!

Upon the next branches of the tree, lower down, hard by the green roller and miniature gardening-tools, how thick the books begin to hang. Thin books, in themselves, at first, but many of them, and with deliciously smooth covers of bright red or green. What fat black letters to begin with! "A was an archer, and shot at a frog." Of course he was. He was an apple-pie also, and there he is! He was a good many things in his time, was A, and so were most of his friends, except X, who had so little versatility, that I never knew him to get beyond Xerxes or Xantippe—like Y, who was always confined to a Yacht or a Yew Tree; and Z condemned for ever to be a Zebra or a Zany. But, now, the very tree itself changes, and becomes a bean-stalk—the marvellous bean-stalk up which Jack climbed to the Giant's house! And now, those dreadfully interesting, double-headed giants, with their clubs over their shoulders, begin to stride along the boughs in a perfect throng, dragging knights and ladies home for dinner by the hair of their heads. And Jack—how noble, with his sword of sharpness, and his shoes of swiftness! Again those old meditations come upon me as I gaze up at him; and I debate within myself whether there was more than one Jack (which I am loth to believe possible), or only one genuine original admirable Jack, who achieved all the recorded exploits.

Good for Christmas-time is the ruddy colour of the cloak, in which—the tree making a forest of itself for her to trip through, with her basket—Little Red Riding-Hood comes to me one Christmas Eve to give me information of the cruelty and treachery of that dissembling Wolf who ate her grandmother, without making any impression on his appetite, and then ate her, after making that ferocious joke about his teeth. She was my first love. I felt that if I could have married Little Red Riding-Hood, I should have known perfect bliss. But, it was not to be; and there was nothing for it but to look out the Wolf in the Noah's Ark there, and put him late in the procession on the table, as a monster who was to be degraded. O the wonderful Noah's Ark! It was not found seaworthy when put in a washing-tub, and the animals were crammed in at the roof, and needed to have their legs well shaken down before they could be got in, even there—and then, ten to one but they began to tumble out at the door, which was but imperfectly fastened with a wire latch—but what was *that* against it! Consider the noble fly, a size or two smaller than the elephant: the lady-bird, the butterfly—all triumphs of art! Consider the goose, whose feet were so small, and whose balance was so indifferent, that he usually tumbled forward, and knocked down all the animal creation. Consider Noah and his family, like idiotic tobacco-stoppers; and how the leopard stuck to warm little fingers; and how the tails of the larger animals used gradually to resolve themselves into frayed bits of string!

Hush! Again a forest, and somebody up in a tree—not Robin Hood, not Valentine, not the Yellow Dwarf (I have passed him and all Mother Bunch's wonders, without mention), but an Eastern King with a glittering scimitar and turban. By Allah! two Eastern Kings, for I see another, looking over his shoulder! Down upon the grass, at the tree's foot, lies the full length of a coal-black Giant, stretched asleep, with his head in a lady's lap; and near them is a glass box, fastened with four locks of shining steel, in which he keeps the lady prisoner when he is awake. I see the four keys at his girdle now. The lady makes signs to the two kings in the tree, who softly descend. It is the setting-in of the bright Arabian Nights.

Oh, now all common things become uncommon and enchanted to me. All lamps are wonderful; all rings are talismans. Common flower-pots are full of treasure, with a little earth scattered on the top; trees are for Ali Baba to hide in; beef-steaks are to throw down into the Valley of Diamonds, that the precious stones may stick to them, and be carried by the eagles to their nests, whence the traders, with loud cries, will scare them. Tarts are made, according to the recipe of the Vizier's son of Bussorah, who turned pastrycook after he was set down in his drawers at the gate of Damascus; cobblers are all Mustaphas, and in the habit of sewing up people cut into four pieces, to whom they are taken blind-fold.

Any iron ring let into stone is the entrance to a cave which only waits for the magician, and the little fire, and the necromancy, that will make the earth shake. All the dates imported come from the same tree as that unlucky date, with whose shell the merchant knocked out the eye of the genie's invisible son. All olives are of the stock of that fresh fruit, concerning which the Commander of the Faithful overheard the boy conduct the fictitious trial of the fraudulent olive merchant; all apples are akin to the apple purchased (with two others) from the Sultan's gardener for three sequins, and which the tall black slave stole from the child. All dogs are associated with the dog, really a transformed man, who jumped upon the baker's counter, and put his paw on the piece of bad money. All rice recalls the rice which the awful lady, who was a ghoule, could only peck by grains, because of her nightly feasts in the burial-place. My very rocking-horse,—there he is, with his nostrils turned completely inside-out, indicative of Blood!—should have a peg in his neck, by virtue thereof to fly away with me, as the wooden horse did with the Prince of Persia, in the sight of all his father's Court.

Yes, on every object that I recognise among those upper branches of my Christmas Tree, I see this fairy light! When I wake in bed, at daybreak, on the cold, dark, winter mornings, the white snow dimly beheld, outside, through the frost on the window-pane, I hear Dinarzade. "Sister, sister, if you are yet awake, I pray you finish the history of the Young King of the Black Islands." Scheherazade replies, "If my lord the Sultan will suffer me to live another day, sister, I will not only finish that, but tell you a more wonderful story yet." Then, the gracious Sultan goes out, giving no orders for the execution, and we all three breathe again.

At this height of my tree I begin to see, cowering among the leaves—it may be born of turkey, or of pudding, or mince pie, or of these many fancies, jumbled with Robinson Crusoe on his desert island, Philip Quarll among the monkeys, Sandford and Merton with Mr. Barlow, Mother Bunch, and the Mask—or it may be the result of indigestion, assisted by imagination and over-doctoring—a prodigious nightmare. It is so exceedingly indistinct, that I don't know why it's frightful—but I know it is. I can only make out that it is an immense array of shapeless things, which appear to be planted on a vast exaggeration of the lazy-tongs that used to bear the toy soldiers, and to be slowly coming close to my eyes, and receding to an immeasurable distance. When it comes closest, it is worse. In connection with it I descry remembrances of winter nights incredibly long; of being sent early to bed, as a punishment for some small offence, and waking in two hours, with a sensation of having been asleep two nights; of the laden hopelessness of morning ever dawning; and the oppression of a weight of remorse.

And now, I see a wonderful row of little lights rise smoothly out of the ground, before a vast green curtain. Now, a bell rings—a magic bell, which still sounds in my ears unlike all other bells—and music plays, amidst a buzz of voices, and a fragrant smell of orange-peel and oil. Anon, the magic bell commands the music to cease, and the great green curtain rolls itself up majestically, and The Play begins! The devoted dog of Montargis avenges the death of his master, foully murdered in the Forest of Bondy; and a humorous Peasant with a red nose and a very little hat, whom I take from this hour forth to my bosom as a friend (I think he was a Waiter or an Hostler at a village Inn, but many years have passed since he and I have met), remarks that the sassigassity of that dog is indeed surprising; and evermore this jocular conceit will live in my remembrance fresh and unfading, overtopping all possible jokes, unto the end of time. Or now, I learn with bitter tears how poor Jane Shore, dressed all in white, and with her brown hair hanging down, went starving through the streets; or how George Barnwell killed the worthiest uncle that ever man had, and was afterwards so sorry for it that he ought to have been let off. Comes swift to comfort me, the Pantomime—stupendous Phenomenon!—when clowns are shot from loaded mortars into the great chandelier, bright constellation that it is; when Harlequins, covered all over with scales of pure gold, twist and sparkle, like amazing fish; when Pantaloon (whom I deem it no irreverence to compare in my own mind to my grandfather) puts red-hot pokers in his pocket, and cries "Here's somebody coming!" or taxes the Clown with petty larceny, by saying, "Now, I sawed you do it!" when Everything is capable, with the greatest ease, of being changed into Anything; and "Nothing is, but thinking makes it so." Now, too, I perceive my first experience of the dreary sensation—often to return in after-life—of being unable, next day, to get back to the dull, settled world; of wanting to live for ever in the bright atmosphere I have quitted; of doting on the little Fairy, with the wand like a celestial Barber's Pole, and pining for a Fairy immortality along with her. Ah, she comes back, in many shapes, as my eye wanders down the branches of my Christmas Tree, and goes as often, and has never yet stayed by me!

Out of this delight springs the toy-theatre,—there it is, with its familiar proscenium, and ladies in feathers, in the boxes!—and all its attendant occupation with paste and glue, and gum, and water colours, in the getting-up of The Miller and his Men, and Elizabeth, or the Exile of Siberia. In spite of a few besetting accidents and failures (particularly an unreasonable disposition in the respectable Kelmar, and some others, to become faint in the legs, and double up, at exciting points of the drama), a teeming world of fancies so suggestive and all-embracing, that, far below it on my Christmas Tree, I see dark, dirty, real Theatres in the day-time, adorned with these associations as with the freshest garlands of the rarest flowers, and charming me yet.

But hark! The Waits are playing, and they break my childish sleep! What images do I associate with the Christmas music as I see them set forth on the Christmas Tree? Known before all the others, keeping far apart from all the others, they gather round my little bed. An angel, speaking to a group of shepherds in a field; some travellers, with eyes uplifted, following a star; a baby in a manger; a child in a spacious temple, talking with grave men; a solemn figure, with a mild and beautiful face, raising a dead girl by the hand; again, near a city gate, calling back the son of a widow, on his bier, to life; a crowd of people looking through the opened roof of a chamber where he sits, and letting down a sick person on a bed, with ropes; the same, in a tempest, walking on the water to a ship; again, on a sea-shore, teaching a great multitude; again, with a child upon his knee, and other children round; again, restoring sight to the blind, speech to the dumb, hearing to the deaf, health to the sick, strength to the lame, knowledge to the ignorant; again, dying upon a Cross, watched by armed soldiers, a thick darkness coming on, the earth beginning to shake, and only one voice heard, "Forgive them, for they know not what they do."

Still, on the lower and maturer branches of the Tree, Christmas associations cluster thick. School-books shut up; Ovid and Virgil silenced; the Rule of Three, with its cool impertinent inquiries, long disposed of; Terence and Plautus acted no more, in an arena of huddled desks and forms, all chipped, and notched, and inked; cricket-bats, stumps, and balls, left higher up, with the smell of trodden grass and the softened noise of shouts in the evening air; the tree is still fresh, still gay. If I no more come home at Christmas-time, there will be boys and girls (thank Heaven!) while the World lasts; and they do! Yonder they dance and play upon the branches of my Tree, God bless them, merrily, and my heart dances and plays too!

And I do come home at Christmas. We all do, or we all should. We all come home, or ought to come home, for a short holiday—the longer, the better—from the great boarding-school, where we are for ever working at our arithmetical slates, to take, and give a rest. As to going a visiting, where can we not go, if we will; where have we not been, when we would; starting our fancy from our Christmas Tree!

Away into the winter prospect. There are many such upon the tree! On, by low-lying, misty grounds, through fens and fogs, up long hills, winding dark as caverns between thick plantations, almost shutting out the sparkling stars; so, out on broad heights, until we stop at last, with sudden silence, at an avenue. The gate-bell has a deep, half-awful sound in the frosty air; the gate swings open on its hinges; and, as we drive up to a great house, the glancing lights grow larger in the windows, and the opposing rows of trees seem to fall solemnly back on either side, to give us place. At intervals, all day, a frightened hare has shot across this whitened turf; or the distant clatter of a herd of deer trampling the hard frost, has, for the minute, crushed the silence too. Their watchful eyes beneath the fern may be shining now, if we could see them, like the icy dewdrops on the leaves; but they are still, and all is still. And so, the lights growing larger, and the trees falling back before us, and closing up again behind us, as if to forbid retreat, we come to the house.

There is probably a smell of roasted chestnuts and other good comfortable things all the time, for we are telling Winter Stories—Ghost Stories, or more shame for us—round the Christmas fire; and we have never stirred, except to draw a little nearer to it. But, no matter for that. We came to the house, and it is an old house, full of great chimneys where wood is burnt on ancient dogs upon the hearth, and grim portraits (some of them with grim legends, too) lower distrustfully from the oaken panels of the walls. We are a middle-aged nobleman, and we make a generous supper with our host and hostess and their guests—it being Christmas-time, and the old house full of company—and then we go to bed. Our room is a very old room. It is hung with tapestry. We don't like the portrait of a cavalier in green, over the fireplace. There are great black beams in the ceiling, and there is a great black bedstead, supported at the foot by two great black figures, who seem to have come off a couple of tombs in the old baronial church in the park, for our particular accommodation. But, we are not a superstitious nobleman, and we don't mind. Well! we dismiss our servant, lock the door, and sit before the fire in our dressing-gown, musing about a great many things. At length we go to bed. Well! we can't sleep. We toss and tumble, and can't sleep. The embers on the hearth burn fitfully and make the room look ghostly. We can't help peeping out over the counterpane, at the two black figures and the cavalier—that wicked-looking cavalier—in green. In the flickering light they seem to advance and retire: which, though we are not by any means a superstitious nobleman, is not agreeable. Well! we get nervous—more and more nervous. We say "This is very foolish, but we can't stand this; we'll pretend to be ill, and knock up somebody." Well! we are just going to do it, when the locked door opens, and there comes in a young woman, deadly pale, and with long fair hair, who glides to the fire, and sits down in the chair we have left there, wringing her hands. Then, we notice that her clothes are wet. Our tongue cleaves to the roof of our mouth, and we can't speak; but, we observe her accurately. Her clothes are wet; her long hair is dabbled with moist mud; she is dressed in the fashion of two hundred years ago; and she has at her girdle a bunch of rusty keys. Well! there she sits, and we can't even faint, we are in such a state about it. Presently she gets up, and tries all the locks in the room with the rusty keys, which won't fit one of them; then, she fixes her eyes on the portrait of the cavalier in green, and says, in a low, terrible voice, "The stags know it!" After that, she wrings her hands again, passes the bedside, and goes out at the door. We hurry on our dressing-gown, seize our pistols (we always travel with pistols), and are following, when we find the door locked. We turn the key, look out into the dark gallery; no one there. We wander away, and try to find our servant. Can't be done. We pace the gallery till daybreak; then return to our deserted room, fall asleep, and are awakened by our servant (nothing ever haunts him) and the shining sun. Well! we make a wretched breakfast, and all the company say we look queer. After breakfast, we go over the house with our host, and then we take him to the portrait of the cavalier in green, and then it all comes out. He was false to a young housekeeper once attached to that family, and famous for her beauty, who drowned herself in a pond, and whose body was discovered, after a long time, because the stags refused to drink of the water. Since which, it has been whispered that she traverses the house at midnight (but goes especially to that room where the cavalier in green was wont to sleep), trying the old locks with the rusty keys. Well! we tell our host of what we have seen, and a shade comes over his features, and he begs it may be hushed up; and so it is. But, it's all true; and we said so, before we died (we are dead now) to many responsible people.

There is no end to the old houses, with resounding galleries, and dismal state-bedchambers, and haunted wings shut up for many years, through which we may ramble, with an agreeable creeping up our back, and encounter any number of ghosts, but (it is worthy of remark perhaps) reducible to a very few general types and classes; for, ghosts have little originality, and "walk" in a beaten track. Thus, it comes to pass, that a certain room in a certain old hall, where a certain bad lord, baronet, knight, or gentleman, shot himself, has certain planks in the floor from which the blood *will not* be taken out. You may scrape and scrape, as the present owner has done, or plane and plane, as his father did, or scrub and scrub, as his grandfather did, or burn and burn with strong acids, as his great-grandfather did, but, there the blood will still be—no redder and no paler—no more and no less—always just the same. Thus, in such another house there is a haunted door, that never will keep open; or another door that never will keep shut, or a haunted sound of a spinning-wheel, or a hammer, or a footstep, or a cry, or a sigh, or a horse's tramp, or the rattling of a chain. Or else, there is a turret-clock, which, at the midnight hour, strikes thirteen when the head of the family is going to die; or a shadowy, immovable black carriage which at such a time is always seen by somebody, waiting near the great gates in the stable-yard. Or thus, it came to pass how Lady Mary went to pay a visit at a large wild house in the Scottish Highlands, and, being fatigued with her long journey, retired to bed early, and innocently said, next morning, at the breakfast-table, "How odd, to have so late a party last night, in this remote place, and not to tell me of it, before I went to bed!" Then, every one asked Lady Mary what she meant? Then, Lady Mary replied, "Why, all night long, the carriages were driving round and round the terrace, underneath my window!" Then, the owner of the house turned pale, and so did his Lady, and Charles Macdoodle of Macdoodle signed to Lady Mary to say no more, and every one was silent. After breakfast, Charles Macdoodle told Lady Mary that it was a tradition in the family that those rumbling carriages on the terrace betokened death. And so it proved, for, two months afterwards, the Lady of the mansion died. And Lady Mary, who was a Maid of Honour at Court, often told this story to the old Queen Charlotte; by this token that the old King always said, "Eh, eh? What, what? Ghosts, ghosts? No such thing, no such thing!" And never left off saying so, until he went to bed.

Or, a friend of somebody's whom most of us know, when he was a young man at college, had a particular friend, with whom he made the compact that, if it were possible for the Spirit to return to this earth after its separation from the body, he of the twain who first died, should reappear to the other. In course of time, this compact was forgotten by our friend; the two young men having progressed in life, and taken diverging paths that were wide asunder. But, one night, many years afterwards, our friend being in the North of England, and staying for the night in an inn, on the Yorkshire Moors, happened to look out of bed; and there, in the moonlight, leaning on a bureau near the window, steadfastly regarding him, saw his old college friend! The appearance being solemnly addressed, replied, in a kind of whisper, but very audibly, "Do not come near me. I am dead. I am here to redeem my promise. I come from another world, but may not disclose its secrets!" Then, the whole form becoming paler, melted, as it were, into the moonlight, and faded away.

Or, there was the daughter of the first occupier of the picturesque Elizabethan house, so famous in our neighbourhood. You have heard about her? No! Why, *She* went out one summer evening at twilight, when she was a beautiful girl, just seventeen years of age, to gather flowers in the garden; and presently came running, terrified, into the hall to her father, saying, "Oh, dear father, I have met myself!" He took her in his arms, and told her it was fancy, but she said, "Oh no! I met myself in the broad walk, and I was pale and gathering withered flowers, and I turned my head, and held them up!" And, that night, she died; and a picture of her story was begun, though never finished, and they say it is somewhere in the house to this day, with its face to the wall.

Or, the uncle of my brother's wife was riding home on horseback, one mellow evening at sunset, when, in a green lane close to his own house, he saw a man standing before him, in the very centre of a narrow way. "Why does that man in the cloak stand there!" he thought. "Does he want me to ride over him?" But the figure never moved. He felt a strange sensation at seeing it so still, but slackened his trot and rode forward. When he was so close to it, as almost to touch it with his stirrup, his horse shied, and the figure glided up the bank, in a curious, unearthly manner—backward, and without seeming to use its feet—and was gone. The uncle of my brother's wife, exclaiming, "Good Heaven! It's my cousin Harry, from Bombay!" put spurs to his horse, which was suddenly in a profuse sweat, and, wondering at such strange behaviour, dashed round to the front of his house. There, he saw the same figure, just passing in at the long French window of the drawing-room, opening on the ground. He threw his bridle to a servant, and hastened in after it. His sister was sitting there, alone. "Alice, where's my cousin Harry?" "Your cousin Harry, John?" "Yes. From Bombay. I met him in the lane just now, and saw him enter here, this instant." Not a creature had been seen by any one; and in that hour and minute, as it afterwards appeared, this cousin died in India.

Or, it was a certain sensible old maiden lady, who died at ninety-nine, and retained her faculties to the last, who really did see the Orphan Boy; a story which has often been incorrectly told, but, of which the real truth is this—because it is, in fact, a story belonging to our family—and she was a connexion of our family. When she was about forty years of age, and still an uncommonly fine woman (her lover died young, which was the reason why she never married, though she had many offers), she went to stay at a place in Kent, which her brother, an Indian-Merchant, had newly bought. There was a story that this place had once been held in trust by the guardian of a young boy; who was himself the next heir, and who killed the young boy by harsh and cruel treatment. She knew nothing of that. It has been said that there was a Cage in her bedroom in which the guardian used to put the boy. There was no such thing. There was only a closet. She went to bed, made no alarm whatever in the night, and in the morning said composedly to her maid when she came in, "Who is the pretty forlorn-looking child who has been peeping out of that closet all night?" The maid replied by giving a loud scream, and instantly decamping. She was surprised; but she was a woman of remarkable strength of mind, and she dressed herself and went downstairs, and closeted herself with her brother. "Now, Walter," she said, "I have been disturbed all night by a pretty, forlorn-looking boy, who has been constantly peeping out of that closet in my room, which I can't open. This is some trick." "I am afraid not, Charlotte," said he, "for it is the legend of the house. It is the Orphan Boy. What did he do?" "He opened the door softly," said she, "and peeped out. Sometimes, he came a step or two into the room. Then, I called to him, to encourage him, and he shrunk, and shuddered, and crept in again, and shut the door." "The closet has no communication, Charlotte," said her brother, "with any other part of the house, and it's nailed up." This was undeniably true, and it took two carpenters a whole forenoon to get it open, for examination. Then, she was satisfied that she had seen the Orphan Boy. But, the wild and terrible part of the story is, that he was also seen by three of her brother's sons, in succession, who all died young. On the occasion of each child being taken ill, he came home in a heat, twelve hours before, and said, Oh, Mamma, he had been playing under a particular oak-tree, in a certain meadow, with a strange boy—a pretty, forlorn-looking boy, who was very timid, and made signs! From fatal experience, the parents came to know that this was the Orphan Boy, and that the course of that child whom he chose for his little playmate was surely run.

Legion is the name of the German castles, where we sit up alone to wait for the Spectre—where we are shown into a room, made comparatively cheerful for our reception—where we glance round at the shadows, thrown on the blank walls by the crackling fire—where we feel very lonely when the village innkeeper and his pretty daughter have retired, after laying down a fresh store of wood upon the hearth, and setting forth on the small table such supper-cheer as a cold roast capon, bread, grapes, and a flask of old Rhine wine—where the reverberating doors close on their retreat, one after another, like so many peals of sullen thunder—and where, about the small hours of the night, we come into the knowledge of divers supernatural mysteries. Legion is the name of the haunted German students, in whose society we draw yet nearer to the fire, while the schoolboy in the corner opens his eyes wide and round, and flies off the footstool he has chosen for his seat, when the door accidentally blows open. Vast is the crop of such fruit, shining on our Christmas Tree; in blossom, almost at the very top; ripening all down the boughs!

Among the later toys and fancies hanging there—as idle often and less pure—be the images once associated with the sweet old Waits, the softened music in the night, ever unalterable! Encircled by the social thoughts of Christmas-time, still let the benignant figure of my childhood stand unchanged! In every cheerful image and suggestion that the season brings, may the bright star that rested above the poor roof, be the star of all the Christian World! A moment's pause, O vanishing tree, of which the lower boughs are dark to me as yet, and let me look once more! I know there are blank spaces on thy branches, where eyes that I have loved have shone and smiled; from which they are departed. But, far above, I see the raiser of the dead girl, and the Widow's Son; and God is good! If Age be hiding for me in the unseen portion of thy downward growth, O may I, with a grey head, turn a child's heart to that figure yet, and a child's trustfulness and confidence!

Now, the tree is decorated with bright merriment, and song, and dance, and cheerfulness. And they are welcome. Innocent and welcome be they ever held, beneath the branches of the Christmas Tree, which cast no gloomy shadow! But, as it sinks into the ground, I hear a whisper going through the leaves. "This, in commemoration of the law of love and kindness, mercy and compassion. This, in remembrance of Me!"

Mark Twain

A Letter from Santa Claus

Palace of St. Nicholas

In the Moon

Christmas Morning

MY DEAR SUSIE CLEMENS:

I have received and read all the letters which you and your little sister have written me by the hand of your mother and your nurses; I have also read those which you little people have written me with your own hands--for although you did not use any characters that are in grown peoples' alphabet, you used the characters that all children in all lands on earth and in the twinkling stars use; and as all my subjects in the moon are children and use no character but that, you will easily understand that I can read your and your baby sister's jagged and fantastic marks without any trouble at all. But I had trouble with those letters which you dictated through your mother and the nurses, for I am a foreigner and cannot read English writing well. You will find that I made no mistakes about the things which you and the baby ordered in your own letters--I went down your chimney at midnight when you were asleep and delivered them all myself--and kissed both of you, too, because you are good children, well trained, nice mannered, and about the most obedient little people I ever saw. But in the letter which you dictated there were some words which I could not make out for certain, and one or two small orders which I could not fill because we ran out of stock. Our last lot of kitchen furniture for dolls has just gone to a very poor little child in the North Star away up, in the cold country above the Big Dipper. Your mama can show you that star and you will say: "Little Snow Flake," (for that is the child's name) "I'm glad you got that furniture, for you need it more than I." That is, you must write that, with your own hand, and Snow Flake will write you an answer. If you only spoke it she wouldn't hear you. Make your letter light and thin, for the distance is great and the postage very heavy.

There was a word or two in your mama's letter which I couldn't be certain of. I took it to be "a trunk full of doll's clothes." Is that it? I will call at your kitchen door about nine o'clock this morning to inquire. But I must not see anybody and I must not speak to anybody but you. When the kitchen doorbell rings, George must be blindfolded and sent to open the door. Then he must go back to the dining room or the china closet and take the cook with him. You must tell George he must walk on tiptoe and not speak--otherwise he will die someday. Then you must go up to the nursery and stand on a chair or the nurse's bed and put your car to the speaking tube that leads down to the kitchen and when I whistle through it you must speak in the tube and say, "Welcome, Santa Claus!" Then I will ask whether it was a trunk you ordered or not. If you say it was, I shall ask you what color you want the trunk to be. Your mama will help you to name a nice color and then you must tell me every single thing in detail which you want the trunk to contain. Then when I say "Good-by and a merry Christmas to my little Susie Clemens," you must say "Good-by, good old Santa Claus, I thank you very much and please tell that little Snow Flake I will look at her star tonight and she must look down here--I will be right in the west bay window; and every fine night I will look at her star and say, 'I know somebody up there and like her, too.' " Then you must go down into the library and make George close all the doors that open into the main hall, and everybody must keep still for a little while. I will go to the moon and get those things and in a few minutes I will come down the chimney that belongs to the fireplace that is in the hall--if it is a trunk you want--because I couldn't get such a thing as a trunk down the nursery chimney, you know.

People may talk if they want, until they hear my footsteps in the hall. Then you tell them to keep quiet a little while till I go back up the chimney. Maybe you will not hear my footsteps at all--so you may go now and then and peep through the dining-room doors, and by and by you will see that thing which you want, right under the piano in the drawing room-for I shall put it there. If I should leave any snow in the hall, you must tell George to sweep it into the fireplace, for I haven't time to do such things. George must not use a broom, but a rag--else he will die someday. You must watch George and not let him run into danger. If my boot should leave a stain on the marble, George must not holystone it away. Leave it there always in memory of my visit; and whenever you look at it or show it to anybody you must let it remind you to be a good little girl. Whenever you are naughty and somebody points to that mark which your good old Santa Claus's boot made on the marble, what will you say, little sweetheart?

Good-by for a few minutes, till I come down to the world and ring the kitchen doorbell.

Your loving SANTA CLAUS

Whom people sometimes call "The Man in the Moon"

L. Frank Baum

The Life and Adventures of Santa Claus

Contents

YOUTH

MANHOOD

OLD AGE

YOUTH

1. Burzee

Have you heard of the great Forest of Burzee? Nurse used to sing of it when I was a child. She sang of the big tree-trunks, standing close together, with their roots intertwining below the earth and their branches intertwining above it; of their rough coating of bark and queer, gnarled limbs; of the bushy foliage that roofed the entire forest, save where the sunbeams found a path through which to touch the ground in little spots and to cast weird and curious shadows over the mosses, the lichens and the drifts of dried leaves.

The Forest of Burzee is mighty and grand and awesome to those who steal beneath its shade. Coming from the sunlit meadows into its mazes it seems at first gloomy, then pleasant, and afterward filled with never-ending delights.

For hundreds of years it has flourished in all its magnificence, the silence of its inclosure unbroken save by the chirp of busy chipmunks, the growl of wild beasts and the songs of birds.

Yet Burzee has its inhabitants—for all this. Nature peopled it in the beginning with Fairies, Knooks, Ryls and Nymphs. As long as the Forest stands it will be a home, a refuge and a playground to these sweet immortals, who revel undisturbed in its depths.

Civilization has never yet reached Burzee. Will it ever, I wonder?

2. The Child of the Forest

Once, so long ago our great-grandfathers could scarcely have heard it mentioned, there lived within the great Forest of Burzee a wood-nymph named Necile. She was closely related to the mighty Queen Zurline, and her home was beneath the shade of a widespreading oak. Once every year, on Budding Day, when the trees put forth their new buds, Necile held the Golden Chalice of Ak to the lips of the Queen, who drank therefrom to the prosperity of the Forest. So you see she was a nymph of some importance, and, moreover, it is said she was highly regarded because of her beauty and grace.

When she was created she could not have told; Queen Zurline could not have told; the great Ak himself could not have told. It was long ago when the world was new and nymphs were needed to guard the forests and to minister to the wants of the young trees. Then, on some day not remembered, Necile sprang into being; radiant, lovely, straight and slim as the sapling she was created to guard.

Her hair was the color that lines a chestnut-bur; her eyes were blue in the sunlight and purple in the shade; her cheeks bloomed with the faint pink that edges the

rescue them from misery. The men and women I dare not interfere with; they must bear the burdens Nature has imposed upon them. But the helpless infants, the innocent children of men, have a right to be happy until they become full-grown and able to bear the trials of humanity. So I feel I am justified in assisting them. Not long ago—a year, maybe—I found four poor children huddled in a wooden hut, slowly freezing to death. Their parents had gone to a neighboring village for food, and had left a fire to warm their little ones while they were absent. But a storm arose and drifted the snow in their path, so they were long on the road. Meantime the fire went out and the frost crept into the bones of the waiting children."

"Poor things!" murmured the Queen softly. "What did you do?"

"I called Nelko, bidding him fetch wood from my forests and breathe upon it until the fire blazed again and warmed the little room where the children lay. Then they ceased shivering and fell asleep until their parents came."

"I am glad you did thus," said the good Queen, beaming upon the Master; and Necile, who had eagerly listened to every word, echoed in a whisper: "I, too, am glad!"

"And this very night," continued Ak, "as I came to the edge of Burzee I heard a feeble cry, which I judged came from a human infant. I looked about me and found, close to the forest, a helpless babe, lying quite naked upon the grasses and wailing piteously. Not far away, screened by the forest, crouched Shiegra, the lioness, intent upon devouring the infant for her evening meal."

"And what did you do, Ak?" asked the Queen, breathlessly.

"Not much, being in a hurry to greet my nymphs. But I commanded Shiegra to lie close to the babe, and to give it her milk to quiet its hunger. And I told her to send word throughout the forest, to all beasts and reptiles, that the child should not be harmed."

"I am glad you did thus," said the good Queen again, in a tone of relief; but this time Necile did not echo her words, for the nymph, filled with a strange resolve, had suddenly stolen away from the group.

Swiftly her lithe form darted through the forest paths until she reached the edge of mighty Burzee, when she paused to gaze curiously about her. Never until now had she ventured so far, for the Law of the Forest had placed the nymphs in its inmost depths.

Necile knew she was breaking the Law, but the thought did not give pause to her dainty feet. She had decided to see with her own eyes this infant Ak had told of, for she had never yet beheld a child of man. All the immortals are full-grown; there are no children among them. Peering through the trees Necile saw the child lying on the grass. But now it was sweetly sleeping, having been comforted by the milk drawn from Shiegra. It was not old enough to know what peril means; if it did not feel hunger it was content.

Softly the nymph stole to the side of the babe and knelt upon the sward, her long robe of rose leaf color spreading about her like a gossamer cloud. Her lovely countenance expressed curiosity and surprise, but, most of all, a tender, womanly pity. The babe was newborn, chubby and pink. It was entirely helpless. While the nymph gazed the infant opened its eyes, smiled upon her, and stretched out two dimpled arms. In another instant Necile had caught it to her breast and was hurrying with it through the forest paths.

3. The Adoption

The Master Woodsman suddenly rose, with knitted brows. "There is a strange presence in the Forest," he declared. Then the Queen and her nymphs turned and saw standing before them Necile, with the sleeping infant clasped tightly in her arms and a defiant look in her deep blue eyes.

And thus for a moment they remained, the nymphs filled with surprise and consternation, but the brow of the Master Woodsman gradually clearing as he gazed intently upon the beautiful immortal who had wilfully broken the Law. Then the great Ak, to the wonder of all, laid his hand softly on Necile's flowing locks and kissed her on her fair forehead.

"For the first time within my knowledge," said he, gently, "a nymph has defied me and my laws; yet in my heart can I find no word of chiding. What is your desire, Necile?"

"Let me keep the child!" she answered, beginning to tremble and falling on her knees in supplication.

"Here, in the Forest of Burzee, where the human race has never yet penetrated?" questioned Ak.

"Here, in the Forest of Burzee," replied the nymph, boldly. "It is my home, and I am weary for lack of occupation. Let me care for the babe! See how weak and helpless it is. Surely it can not harm Burzee nor the Master Woodsman of the World!"

"But the Law, child, the Law!" cried Ak, sternly.

"The Law is made by the Master Woodsman," returned Necile; "if he bids me care for the babe he himself has saved from death, who in all the world dare oppose me?" Queen Zurline, who had listened intently to this conversation, clapped her pretty hands gleefully at the nymph's answer.

"You are fairly trapped, O Ak!" she exclaimed, laughing. "Now, I pray you, give heed to Necile's petition."

The Woodsman, as was his habit when in thought, stroked his grizzled beard slowly. Then he said:

"She shall keep the babe, and I will give it my protection. But I warn you all that as this is the first time I have relaxed the Law, so shall it be the last time. Never more, to the end of the World, shall a mortal be adopted by an immortal. Otherwise would we abandon our happy existence for one of trouble and anxiety. Good night, my nymphs!"

Then Ak was gone from their midst, and Necile hurried away to her bower to rejoice over her new-found treasure.

4. Claus

Another day found Necile's bower the most popular place in the Forest. The nymphs clustered around her and the child that lay asleep in her lap, with expressions of curiosity and delight. Nor were they wanting in praises for the great Ak's kindness in allowing Necile to keep the babe and to care for it. Even the Queen came to peer into the innocent childish face and to hold a helpless, chubby fist in her own fair hand.

"What shall we call him, Necile?" she asked, smiling. "He must have a name, you know."

"Let him be called Claus," answered Necile, "for that means 'a little one.'"

"Rather let him be called Neclaus,"** returned the Queen, "for that will mean 'Necile's little one.'"

The nymphs clapped their hands in delight, and Neclaus became the infant's name, although Necile loved best to call him Claus, and in afterdays many of her sisters followed her example.

Necile gathered the softest moss in all the forest for Claus to lie upon, and she made his bed in her own bower. Of food the infant had no lack. The nymphs searched the forest for bell-udders, which grow upon the goa-tree and when opened are found to be filled with sweet milk. And the soft-eyed does willingly gave a share of their milk to support the little stranger, while Shiegra, the lioness, often crept stealthily into Necile's bower and purred softly as she lay beside the babe and fed it.

So the little one flourished and grew big and sturdy day by day, while Necile taught him to speak and to walk and to play.

His thoughts and words were sweet and gentle, for the nymphs knew no evil and their hearts were pure and loving. He became the pet of the forest, for Ak's decree had forbidden beast or reptile to molest him, and he walked fearlessly wherever his will guided him.

Presently the news reached the other immortals that the nymphs of Burzee had adopted a human infant, and that the act had been sanctioned by the great Ak. Therefore many of them came to visit the little stranger, looking upon him with much interest. First the Ryls, who are first cousins to the wood-nymphs, although so differently formed. For the Ryls are required to watch over the flowers and plants, as the nymphs watch over the forest trees. They search the wide world for the food required by the roots of the flowering plants, while the brilliant colors possessed by the full-blown flowers are due to the dyes placed in the soil by the Ryls, which are drawn through the little veins in the roots and the body of the plants, as they reach maturity. The Ryls are a busy people, for their flowers bloom and fade continually, but they are merry and light-hearted and are very popular with the other immortals.

Next came the Knooks, whose duty it is to watch over the beasts of the world, both gentle and wild. The Knooks have a hard time of it, since many of the beasts are ungovernable and rebel against restraint. But they know how to manage them, after all, and you will find that certain laws of the Knooks are obeyed by even the most ferocious animals. Their anxieties make the Knooks look old and worn and crooked, and their natures are a bit rough from associating with wild creatures continually; yet they are most useful to humanity and to the world in general, as their laws are the only laws the forest beasts recognize except those of the Master Woodsman.

Then there were the Fairies, the guardians of mankind, who were much interested in the adoption of Claus because their own laws forbade them to become familiar with their human charges. There are instances on record where the Fairies have shown themselves to human beings, and have even conversed with them; but they are supposed to guard the lives of mankind unseen and unknown, and if they favor some people more than others it is because these have won such distinction fairly, as the Fairies are very just and impartial. But the idea of adopting a child of men had never occurred to them because it was in every way opposed to their laws; so their curiosity was intense to behold the little stranger adopted by Necile and her sister nymphs.

Claus looked upon the immortals who thronged around him with fearless eyes and smiling lips. He rode laughingly upon the shoulders of the merry Ryls; he mischievously pulled the gray beards of the low-browed Knooks; he rested his curly head confidently upon the dainty bosom of the Fairy Queen herself. And the Ryls loved the sound of his laughter; the Knooks loved his courage; the Fairies loved his innocence.

The boy made friends of them all, and learned to know their laws intimately. No forest flower was trampled beneath his feet, lest the friendly Ryls should be grieved. He never interfered with the beasts of the forest, lest his friends the Knooks should become angry. The Fairies he loved dearly, but, knowing nothing of mankind, he could not understand that he was the only one of his race admitted to friendly intercourse with them.

Indeed, Claus came to consider that he alone, of all the forest people, had no like nor fellow. To him the forest was the world. He had no idea that millions of toiling, striving human creatures existed.

And he was happy and content.

** Some people have spelled this name Nicklaus and others Nicolas, which is the reason that Santa Claus is still known in some lands as St. Nicolas. But, of course, Neclaus is his right name, and Claus the nickname given him by his adopted mother, the fair nymph Necile.

5. The Master Woodsman

Years pass swiftly in Burzee, for the nymphs have no need to regard time in any way. Even centuries make no change in the dainty creatures; ever and ever they remain the same, immortal and unchanging.

Claus, however, being mortal, grew to manhood day by day. Necile was disturbed, presently, to find him too big to lie in her lap, and he had a desire for other food than milk. His stout legs carried him far into Burzee's heart, where he gathered supplies of nuts and berries, as well as several sweet and wholesome roots, which suited his stomach better than the belludders. He sought Necile's bower less frequently, till finally it became his custom to return thither only to sleep.

The nymph, who had come to love him dearly, was puzzled to comprehend the changed nature of her charge, and unconsciously altered her own mode of life to conform to his whims. She followed him readily through the forest paths, as did many of her sister nymphs, explaining as they walked all the mysteries of the gigantic wood and the habits and nature of the living things which dwelt beneath its shade.

The language of the beasts became clear to little Claus; but he never could understand their sulky and morose tempers. Only the squirrels, the mice and the rabbits seemed to possess cheerful and merry natures; yet would the boy laugh when the panther growled, and stroke the bear's glossy coat while the creature snarled and bared its teeth menacingly. The growls and snarls were not for Claus, he well knew, so what did they matter?

He could sing the songs of the bees, recite the poetry of the wood-flowers and relate the history of every blinking owl in Burzee. He helped the Ryls to feed their plants and the Knooks to keep order among the animals. The little immortals regarded him as a privileged person, being especially protected by Queen Zurline and her nymphs and favored by the great Ak himself.

One day the Master Woodsman came back to the forest of Burzee. He had visited, in turn, all his forests throughout the world, and they were many and broad.

Not until he entered the glade where the Queen and her nymphs were assembled to greet him did Ak remember the child he had permitted Necile to adopt. Then he found, sitting familiarly in the circle of lovely immortals, a broad-shouldered, stalwart youth, who, when erect, stood fully as high as the shoulder of the Master himself.

Ak paused, silent and frowning, to bend his piercing gaze upon Claus. The clear eyes met his own steadfastly, and the Woodsman gave a sigh of relief as he marked their placid depths and read the youth's brave and innocent heart. Nevertheless, as Ak sat beside the fair Queen, and the golden chalice, filled with rare nectar, passed from lip to lip, the Master Woodsman was strangely silent and reserved, and stroked his beard many times with a thoughtful motion.

With morning he called Claus aside, in kindly fashion, saying:

"Bid good by, for a time, to Necile and her sisters; for you shall accompany me on my journey through the world."

The venture pleased Claus, who knew well the honor of being companion of the Master Woodsman of the world. But Necile wept for the first time in her life, and clung to the boy's neck as if she could not bear to let him go. The nymph who had mothered this sturdy youth was still as dainty, as charming and beautiful as when she had dared to face Ak with the babe clasped to her breast; nor was her love less great. Ak beheld the two clinging together, seemingly as brother and sister to one another, and again he wore his thoughtful look.

6. Claus Discovers Humanity

Taking Claus to a small clearing in the forest, the Master said: "Place your hand upon my girdle and hold fast while we journey through the air; for now shall we encircle the world and look upon many of the haunts of those men from whom you are descended."

These words caused Claus to marvel, for until now he had thought himself the only one of his kind upon the earth; yet in silence he grasped firmly the girdle of the great Ak, his astonishment forbidding speech.

Then the vast forest of Burzee seemed to fall away from their feet, and the youth found himself passing swiftly through the air at a great height.

Ere long there were spires beneath them, while buildings of many shapes and colors met their downward view. It was a city of men, and Ak, pausing to descend, led Claus to its inclosure. Said the Master:

"So long as you hold fast to my girdle you will remain unseen by all mankind, though seeing clearly yourself. To release your grasp will be to separate yourself forever from me and your home in Burzee."

One of the first laws of the Forest is obedience, and Claus had no thought of disobeying the Master's wish. He clung fast to the girdle and remained invisible.

Thereafter with each moment passed in the city the youth's wonder grew. He, who had supposed himself created differently from all others, now found the earth swarming with creatures of his own kind.

"Indeed," said Ak, "the immortals are few; but the mortals are many."

Claus looked earnestly upon his fellows. There were sad faces, gay and reckless faces, pleasant faces, anxious faces and kindly faces, all mingled in puzzling disorder. Some worked at tedious tasks; some strutted in impudent conceit; some were thoughtful and grave while others seemed happy and content. Men of many natures were there, as everywhere, and Claus found much to please him and much to make him sad.

But especially he noted the children—first curiously, then eagerly, then lovingly. Ragged little ones rolled in the dust of the streets, playing with scraps and pebbles. Other children, gaily dressed, were propped upon cushions and fed with sugar-plums. Yet the children of the rich were not happier than those playing with the dust and pebbles, it seemed to Claus.

"Childhood is the time of man's greatest content," said Ak, following the youth's thoughts. "'Tis during these years of innocent pleasure that the little ones are most free from care."

"Tell me," said Claus, "why do not all these babies fare alike?"

"Because they are born in both cottage and palace," returned the Master. "The difference in the wealth of the parents determines the lot of the child. Some are carefully tended and clothed in silks and dainty linen; others are neglected and covered with rags."

"Yet all seem equally fair and sweet," said Claus, thoughtfully.

"While they are babes—yes;" agreed Ak. "Their joy is in being alive, and they do not stop to think. In after years the doom of mankind overtakes them, and they find they must struggle and worry, work and fret, to gain the wealth that is so dear to the hearts of men. Such things are unknown in the Forest where you were reared." Claus was silent a moment. Then he asked:

"Why was I reared in the forest, among those who are not of my race?"

Then Ak, in gentle voice, told him the story of his babyhood: how he had been abandoned at the forest's edge and left a prey to wild beasts, and how the loving nymph Necile had rescued him and brought him to manhood under the protection of the immortals.

"Yet I am not of them," said Claus, musingly.

"You are not of them," returned the Woodsman. "The nymph who cared for you as a mother seems now like a sister to you; by and by, when you grow old and gray, she will seem like a daughter. Yet another brief span and you will be but a memory, while she remains Necile."

"Then why, if man must perish, is he born?" demanded the boy.

"Everything perishes except the world itself and its keepers," answered Ak. "But while life lasts everything on earth has its use. The wise seek ways to be helpful to the world, for the helpful ones are sure to live again."

Much of this Claus failed to understand fully, but a longing seized him to become helpful to his fellows, and he remained grave and thoughtful while they resumed their journey.

They visited many dwellings of men in many parts of the world, watching farmers toil in the fields, warriors dash into cruel fray, and merchants exchange their goods for bits of white and yellow metal. And everywhere the eyes of Claus sought out the children in love and pity, for the thought of his own helpless babyhood was strong within him and he yearned to give help to the innocent little ones of his race even as he had been succored by the kindly nymph.

Day by day the Master Woodsman and his pupil traversed the earth, Ak speaking but seldom to the youth who clung steadfastly to his girdle, but guiding him into all places where he might become familiar with the lives of human beings.

And at last they returned to the grand old Forest of Burzee, where the Master set Claus down within the circle of nymphs, among whom the pretty Necile anxiously awaited him.

The brow of the great Ak was now calm and peaceful; but the brow of Claus had become lined with deep thought. Necile sighed at the change in her foster-son, who until now had been ever joyous and smiling, and the thought came to her that never again would the life of the boy be the same as before this eventful journey with the Master.

7. Claus Leaves the Forest

When good Queen Zurline had touched the golden chalice with her fair lips and it had passed around the circle in honor of the travelers' return, the Master

POEMS

Henry Wadsworth Longfellow

Christmas Bells

I heard the bells on Christmas Day
Their old, familiar carols play,
and wild and sweet
The words repeat
Of peace on earth, good-will to men!

And thought how, as the day had come,
The belfries of all Christendom
Had rolled along
The unbroken song
Of peace on earth, good-will to men!

Till ringing, singing on its way,
The world revolved from night to day,
A voice, a chime,
A chant sublime
Of peace on earth, good-will to men!

Then from each black, accursed mouth
The cannon thundered in the South,
And with the sound
The carols drowned

Of peace on earth, good-will to men!

It was as if an earthquake rent
The hearth-stones of a continent,
And made forlorn
The households born
Of peace on earth, good-will to men!

And in despair I bowed my head;
"There is no peace on earth," I said;
"For hate is strong,
And mocks the song
Of peace on earth, good-will to men!"

Then pealed the bells more loud and deep:
"God is not dead, nor doth He sleep;
The Wrong shall fail,
The Right prevail,
With peace on earth, good-will to men."

Eliza Cook

Christmas Tide

When the merry spring time weaves
Its peeping bloom and dewy leaves;
When the primrose opes its eye,
And the young moth flutters by;
When the plaintive turtle dove
Pours its notes of peace and love;
And the clear sun flings its glory bright and wide—
Yet, my soul will own
More joy in winter's frown,
And wake with warmer flush at Christmas tide.

The summer beams may shine
On the rich and curling vine,
And the noon-tide rays light up

The tulip's dazzling cup:
But the pearly misletoe
And the holly-berries' glow
Are not even by the boasted rose outvied;
For the happy hearts beneath
The green and coral wreath
Love the garlands that are twined at Christmas tide.

Let the autumn days produce
Yellow corn and purple juice,
And Nature's feast be spread
In the fruitage ripe and red;
'Tis grateful to behold
Gushing grapes and fields of gold,
When cheeks are brown'd and red lips deeper dyed:
But give, oh! give to me
The winter night of glee,
The mirth and plenty seen at Christmas tide.

The northern gust may howl,

The rolling storm-cloud scowl,
King Frost may make a slave
Of the river's rapid wave,
The snow-drift choke the path,
Or the hail-shower spend its wrath;
But the sternest blast right bravely is defied,
While limbs and spirits bound
To the merry minstrel sound,
And social wood-fires blaze at Christmas tide.

The song, the laugh, the shout,
Shall mock the storm without;
And sparkling wine-foam rise
'Neath still more sparkling eyes;
The forms that rarely meet
Then hand to hand shall greet,
And soul pledge soul that leagues too long divide.
Mirth, friendship, love, and light
Shall crown the winter night,
And every glad voice welcome Christmas tide.

But while joy's echo falls
In gay and plenteous halls,
Let the poor and lowly share
The warmth, the sports, the fare;
For the one of humble lot
Must not shiver in his cot,
But claim a bounteous meed from wealth and pride.
Shed kindly blessings round,
Till no aching heart be found;
And then all hail to merry Christmas tide!

Samuel Taylor Coleridge

A Christmas Carol

I.

The shepherds went their hasty way,

And found the lowly stable-shed

Where the Virgin-Mother lay:

And now they checked their eager tread,

For to the Babe, that at her bosom clung,

A Mother's song the Virgin-Mother sung.

II.

They told her how a glorious light,

Streaming from a heavenly throng.

Around them shone, suspending night!

While sweeter than a mother's song,

Blest Angels heralded the Savior's birth,

Glory to God on high! and Peace on Earth.

III.

She listened to the tale divine,

And closer still the Babe she pressed:

And while she cried, the Babe is mine!

The milk rushed faster to her breast:

Joy rose within her, like a summer's morn;

Peace, Peace on Earth! the Prince of Peace is born.

IV.

Thou Mother of the Prince of Peace,

Poor, simple, and of low estate!

That strife should vanish, battle cease,

O why should this thy soul elate?

Sweet Music's loudest note, the Poet's story,

Didst thou ne'er love to hear of fame and glory?

V.

And is not War a youthful king,

A stately Hero clad in mail?

Beneath his footsteps laurels spring;

Him Earth's majestic monarchs hail

Their friends, their playmate! and his bold bright eye

Compels the maiden's love-confessing sigh.

VI.

Tell this in some more courtly scene,

To maids and youths in robes of state!

I am a woman poor and mean,

And wherefore is my soul elate.

War is a ruffian, all with guilt defiled,

That from the aged father's tears his child!

VII.

A murderous fiend, by fiends adored,

He kills the sire and starves the son;

The husband kills, and from her board

Steals all his widow's toil had won;

Plunders God's world of beauty; rends away

All safety from the night, all comfort from the day.

VIII.

Then wisely is my soul elate,

That strife should vanish, battle cease:

I'm poor and of low estate,

The Mother of the Prince of Peace.

Joy rises in me, like a summer's morn:

Peace, Peace on Earth! The Prince of Peace is born!

Anne Brontë

Music on Christmas Morning

Music I love -- but never strain

Could kindle raptures so divine,

So grief assuage, so conquer pain,

And rouse this pensive heart of mine --

As that we hear on Christmas morn,

Upon the wintry breezes borne.

Though Darkness still her empire keep,

And hours must pass, ere morning break;

From troubled dreams, or slumbers deep,

That music kindly bids us wake:

It calls us, with an angel's voice,

To wake, and worship, and rejoice;

To greet with joy the glorious morn,

Which angels welcomed long ago,

When our redeeming Lord was born,
To bring the light of Heaven below;
The Powers of Darkness to dispel,
And rescue Earth from Death and Hell.

While listening to that sacred strain,
My raptured spirit soars on high;
I seem to hear those songs again
Resounding through the open sky,
That kindled such divine delight,
In those who watched their flocks by night.

With them, I celebrate His birth --
Glory to God, in highest Heaven,
Good-will to men, and peace on Earth,
To us a Saviour-king is given;
Our God is come to claim His own,
And Satan's power is overthrown!

A sinless God, for sinful men,

Descends to suffer and to bleed;
Hell must renounce its empire then;
The price is paid, the world is freed,
And Satan's self must now confess,
That Christ has earned a Right to bless:

Now holy Peace may smile from heaven,
And heavenly Truth from earth shall spring:
The captive's galling bonds are riven,
For our Redeemer is our king;
And He that gave his blood for men
Will lead us home to God again.

Alfred Lord Tennyson

Ring Out, Wild Bells

Ring out, wild bells, to the wild sky,
The flying cloud, the frosty light:
The year is dying in the night;
Ring out, wild bells, and let him die.

Ring out the old, ring in the new,
Ring, happy bells, across the snow:
The year is going, let him go;
Ring out the false, ring in the true.

Ring out the grief that saps the mind
For those that here we see no more;
Ring out the feud of rich and poor,
Ring in redress to all mankind.

Ring out a slowly dying cause,
And ancient forms of party strife;
Ring in the nobler modes of life,
With sweeter manners, purer laws.

Ring out the want, the care, the sin,
The faithless coldness of the times;
Ring out, ring out my mournful rhymes
But ring the fuller minstrel in.

Ring out false pride in place and blood,
The civic slander and the spite;
Ring in the love of truth and right,
Ring in the common love of good.

Ring out old shapes of foul disease;
Ring out the narrowing lust of gold;
Ring out the thousand wars of old,
Ring in the thousand years of peace.

Ring in the valiant man and free,
The larger heart, the kindlier hand;
Ring out the darkness of the land,
Ring in the Christ that is to be.

William Makepeace Thackeray

The Mahogany Tree

Christmas is here;

Winds whistle shrill,

Icy and chill,

Little care we;

Little we fear

Weather without,

Shelter'd about

The Mahogany Tree.

Once on the boughs

Birds of rare plume

Sang, in its bloom;

Night birds are we;

Here we carouse,

Singing, like them,

Perch'd round the stem
Of the jolly old tree.

Here let us sport,
Boys, as we sit—
Laughter and wit
Flashing so free.
Life is but short—
When we are gone,
Let them sing on,
Round the old tree.

Evenings we knew,
Happy as this;
Faces we miss,
Pleasant to see.
Kind hearts and true,
Gentle and just,
Peace to your dust!
We sing round the tree.

Care, like a dun,
Lurks at the gate:
Let the dog wait;
Happy we 'll be!
Drink every one;
Pile up the coals,
Fill the red bowls,
Round the old tree.

Drain we the cup.—
Friend, art afraid?
Spirits are laid
In the Red Sea.
Mantle it up;
Empty it yet;
Let us forget,
Round the old tree.

Sorrows, begone!

Life and its ills,

Duns and their bills,

Bid we to flee.

Come with the dawn,

Blue-devil sprite,

Leave us to-night,

Round the old tree.

Christina Rossetti

Christmas Eve

CHRISTMAS hath darkness
Brighter than the blazing noon,
Christmas hath a chillness
Warmer than the heat of June,
Christmas hath a beauty
Lovelier than the world can show:
For Christmas bringeth Jesus,
Brought for us so low.

Earth, strike up your music,
Birds that sing and bells that ring;
Heaven hath answering music
For all Angels soon to sing:
Earth, put on your whitest

If you enjoyed this book, please leave a review on Amazon

Printed in Great Britain
by Amazon

72018073R00104